A MALMÖ MIDWINTER

An Inspector Anita Sundström mystery

Torquil MacLeod

M^CNIDDER & GRACE CRIME

To Ylva; a special Swedish granddaughter.

Published by McNidder & Grace
Aswarby House
Aswarby
Lincolnshire NG34 8SE

www.mcnidderandgrace.co.uk

Original paperback first published in 2017
©Torquil MacLeod and Torquil MacLeod Books Ltd
www.torquilmacleodbooks.com

A catalogue record for this work is available from the British Library.

ISBN: 9780857161741

Designed by Obsidian Design
Printed in EU by Pulsio Print

ABOUT THE AUTHOR

Torquil MacLeod was born in Edinburgh. After working in advertising agencies in Birmingham, Glasgow and Newcastle, he's now settled in Cumbria with his wife, Susan, and her hens. The idea for a Scandinavian crime series came from his frequent trips to Malmö and southern Sweden to visit his elder son. He now has four grandchildren, two of whom are Swedish.

ACKNOWLEDGEMENTS

I'd like to thank Fraser and Paula for a pleasant research base and Christmas TV information; Karin for her wide-ranging help, accompanied by the usual red wine; Bill and Justine for saving my bacon and a possible court appearance; Linda for her unstinting support and her tireless promotion of The Malmö Mysteries; also not forgetting Nick Pugh at The Roundhouse for another excellent cover design. And to Susan for her rigorous editing – and for not allowing me to get away with inconsistencies.

I would also like to thank all those family, friends and readers who have contacted me and given me the encouragement to continue with the series.

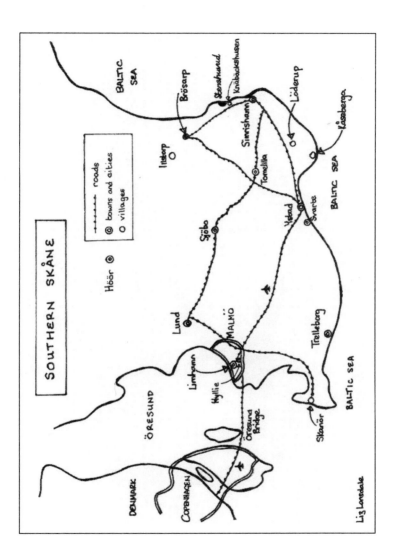

SOUTHERN SKÅNE

roads
towns and cities
villages

BALTIC SEA
ÖRESUND
DENMARK
COPENHAGEN
Öresund Bridge
Skanör
Hyllie
Limhann
MALMÖ
Trelleborg
Lund
Sjöbo
Höör
Tomelilla
Ilstorp
Brösarp
Gärsnäs
Knäbäckshusen
Simrishamn
Löderup
Kåseberga
Ystad
Svarte
BALTIC SEA

Liz Lonsdale

CHAPTER 1

There was nothing. Literally nothing. He was too shocked to react at first. His brain couldn't register what his eyes could see. He had sauntered happily up to his trendily modern apartment block in the shadow of the Turning Torso. He'd had a couple of long days in Stockholm and an afternoon back at the office, and now he was looking forward to unwinding with a few friends at a nearby restaurant. But first, he had promised himself a refreshing shower and a change of clothes. Though he loved his work at the law firm, it was a relief to escape his colleagues, with their constant internal politics and jockeying for position. Stockholm had been a bit of an analgesic. But the job paid handsomely, and its fruits had bought him his stylish home with its panoramic views of the Sound across to Copenhagen, where he could spend his money in the smart restaurants, chic bars and cool boutiques. The apartment, with its designer decor, collectors' items and up-to-the-minute technology, was the most tangible reward for his success at a young age. Life was good. Until the moment he had opened the front door.

The click of his expensive leather-soled shoes on the polished beechwood floor echoed eerily round the empty living room. He had enjoyed furnishing the place – everything several notches above the IKEA trappings he'd grown up with. He'd been so proud of the horrendously pricey Nanna Ditzel easy

1

chair; and his sentimental attachment to the Skagerak mirror his parents had bought him as a house-warming present always brought a smile to his lips. Now there wasn't a stick to be seen. No mounted photographs or investment paintings on the walls, no Chinese rugs on the floor, no *objets d'art*, no wide-screen TV – oh, shit! – the awesome Bang & Olufsen sound system he'd paid a small fortune for had gone, too. He felt bile rising in his throat and he forced it back down before he was physically sick.

The kitchen was the same. All the built-in appliances like the cooker, dishwasher and fridge were still in place, but the microwave was gone, as was his fancy coffee-making machine. The cupboards and drawers had been ignored and the food had been left, but as he rarely ate in, that wasn't much of a consolation. But the wine! The empty racks! He'd spent the whole of his last bonus on starting his collection of bottles from vintages recommended by one of the senior partners. He hardly dared go into the bedroom. The bed was still there, but on opening the walk-in wardrobe, he swore as he saw that his beautiful collection of expensive suits and shirts was missing. Oh, no! – even the Christmas presents he'd spent so long choosing for the family were no longer there. He went to the window, looked out, and saw the bright electric candle Christmas lights in the adjacent apartments poking fun at him. He turned round, leant back against the wall and slowly slid down it until he was sitting on the bare floorboards. He let the tears of frustration and disbelief run freely down his face. How could this have happened?

He wiped his eyes and his lawyer's head took over. He had to marshal the facts. Review the evidence. He had used his own key to get into the apartment. Nothing had been forced. Whoever had removed his belongings hadn't broken in – the burglars must have just waltzed through the front door with a key of their own. No one else had one, except his mother, who lived up the coast in Helsingborg. They didn't always see eye to eye, but she wouldn't have carried any arguments this far. So, who?

He cast his mind back over the last few days. They must have known that he was away in Stockholm and that they wouldn't be disturbed. Half the office was aware of his movements, or they could easily have found out. But who on earth at work could or would have had anything to do with this? And why? He got on with most of his colleagues. OK, he may have rubbed one or two of them up the wrong way. But this? No. There must be a rational explanation. Who else had he told that he would be away? A couple of friends knew, but he quickly dismissed them.

Then it struck him with horrible clarity. The club. The girls.

CHAPTER 2

Murder tends to spoil Christmas. And it wasn't what Inspector Hakim Mirza of the Malmö Criminal Investigation Team was expecting when he had happily agreed to cover for his non-religious colleagues while they enjoyed taking time off work to celebrate the birth of Christ.

It was Christmas Eve; Swedish Yuletide. He had their section of the polishus virtually to himself. Chief Inspector Moberg had found himself a new woman, who had dragged him off reluctantly to the sun in Tenerife. He knew that Moberg hated the heat, but was obviously at the stage in the association where he was making an effort. With three divorces behind him, Hakim wasn't hopeful that this would be a long-lasting relationship – if it made it beyond New Year, he would be surprised. Co-incidentally, his sister Jazmin had probably gone out to Tenerife on the same flight. She and Inspector Anita Sundström's son, Lasse, were spending Christmas out there – a present from Anita, who felt they deserved it after the frightening events of last summer. Anita herself had been unable to avoid spending the festive season – well, three days of it – with her mother, who lived with her unmarried sister in Kristianstad on the other side of Skåne. Hakim smiled at the thought of Anita desperately trying to come up with an excuse not to go, but feeling duty-bound to put up with her mother's constant carping and her aunt's unappetizing

4

cooking. Klara Wallen had gone off somewhere north with her partner, and Pontus Brodd was supposedly "on call" if anything serious happened. Hakim fervently hoped that nothing would come in, as he had little faith in his lethargic colleague's abilities.

As he was sitting at his desk, he opened the file on the case that he and Wallen were currently working on. Three men had had their apartments cleared out. All were young and successful. And all had fallen foul of the same scam, as the interview with Greger Sahlén three days before Christmas had revealed.

Sahlén had become quite reticent when Hakim and Wallen had spoken to him in his virtually empty apartment; a scene that they were starting to get used to. Was this caginess due to the realization that his insurance company might not pay up if the burglars had simply let themselves in? Sahlén couldn't think of anyone who might have committed the crime – or he wasn't keen to tell.

Wallen had let Hakim take the lead. 'You didn't happen to bring two young women back to your apartment a few days before the burglary?'

The startled expression on the lawyer's face confirmed it. Slowly, he nodded.

'OK, what happened?'

Sahlén looked at the bare wall. The faint impression of where a picture had once hung stared back. 'I went to a club. Celebrating. We'd had a good win in court, and I'd had a few drinks at the office before heading out.' His foot found something invisible to scuff. 'A couple of girls came up and started chatting.'

'One long-haired redhead and one bobbed brunette? The redhead of medium height and the other slightly taller?' asked Wallen, without expecting an answer. She held up a sheet of paper with two identikits.

'Can't tell from those. They were young. Well, perhaps early twenties; the brunette might have been younger.' He glanced around the living room. It wasn't going to bring his furniture back, however hard he tried to imagine the pieces in their carefully chosen settings.

'And?' Hakim prompted.

'I bought them drinks. A few drinks, actually.'

'Showing off,' commented Wallen unnecessarily.

'We danced. I thought it would be nice to get off with the redhead. The older one. I fancied her. But I couldn't split them. They seemed to come as a pair. Then when the redhead was in the toilet, the dark girl – I can't remember their names – asked if I was up for a threesome.'

'And, presumably, you weren't going to turn that down,' Wallen said with disdain.

'What guy would? Two lovely girls.'

'Then you came back here?' Hakim knew the scenario, but he needed it to be confirmed.

'Yes. One of them had a bottle of vodka.' Sahlén's face creased up as he was trying to force out the memories. 'And then I don't remember much after that.'

'Did you have sex?'

'I can't fucking remember!' He sounded genuinely exasperated. 'I woke up the next morning feeling like death. It was so annoying. I could have had a great experience, but I couldn't recall a thing.'

'I wouldn't worry about it. You can take it from me that they won't have slept with you.' Wallen was almost triumphant. Why were men like this? she wondered. If Sahlén could have remembered the sex – and be able to boast about it – then he could probably have lived with the subsequent stripping of his apartment; it would have made it all worthwhile.

'Did you mention your Stockholm trip to them?' asked Hakim.

'I don't know. Possibly.'

'Well, you're not the first. In fact, you're the third that we know about. Men being chatted up by a young brunette and an older redhead.' The descriptions of the girls – other than the hair – had been equivocal to say the least. Not surprisingly, the computer representations hadn't produced any positive leads. The CCTV footage from the clubs had shown them leaving with their two previous victims, but the pictures were obscure and enigmatic; they could have been anybody. 'They go back to the apartment, produce a bottle of vodka, which is spiked, probably with something like Rohypnol; the man flakes out, and the girls take impressions of his house keys. But they've also wheedled information out of their mark about his movements, so they know when the coast will be clear and the gang can move in. In your case, I expect you told them about your Stockholm trip.'

'Oh, God! I can't believe how stupid I've been!'

For a fleeting second, even Wallen felt sorry for him.

Hakim looked over the extensive inventory that Sahlén had provided of his stolen items. They had little to go on. The facial descriptions of the girls provided by all three victims had been equally unhelpful. But what the police did have on this occasion was a sighting of a green transit van near Sahlén's apartment block the day that his possessions were moved out. Two young men had been spotted. Again, the report was vague and from a single source, as the burglary had been carried out in the middle of the day when few people were around – and those that were weren't very forthcoming; Swedes like to mind their own business. Hakim closed the file and glanced over to the window. It was snowing. He got up and went over to look. The snowflakes were large and falling fast. The grassed area opposite, illuminated by the street lamps along Kungsgatan, was almost white already. The first serious fall this winter. He was disturbed by the phone ringing. He instinctively looked at his watch. It was a quarter past five. *Jultomten* would have arrived in millions of Swedish homes at around four – after the end of *Donald Duck and Friends*, a Disney compilation which was on

TV every year to distract the kids until the magic hour – and would have handed out presents. The little, mischievous sprite of legend had, over time, morphed into the modern adult wearing a Santa Claus suit, crying out: 'Are there any good children here?' A time of excitement, wonder and joy. He picked up the receiver. The last thing he wanted was to be called out to an incident in this weather. His brow furrowed as he listened.

'I'll be there as soon as I can.'

He put down the phone. It sounded like there was now one less *tomten*.

CHAPTER 3

Hakim wasn't the most confident of drivers as he didn't own a vehicle, nor had he cause to drive a pool car that often. He usually went out with Anita or Wallen, and they both preferred to be behind the wheel. Given that the snow was sudden and that many of the commune workers were on holiday, the roads were becoming difficult to navigate. The windscreen wipers fought bravely against the bombarding flakes. Everything around him disappeared in a niveous haze as he left the urban fringes of Malmö. He latched on to a large Saab in front and followed its red tail lights. He had wondered whether he should have rung Brodd before he left headquarters, but had quickly dismissed the notion. Brodd would be more of a hindrance. He would assess the situation first before calling for extra help. He knew that there would be a couple of local constables on the spot when he got there. It was probably a simple domestic, and the culprit would be obvious; a family row leading to someone going too far, with fatal consequences.

Fortunately, much to his relief, as he approached his destination, the snow began to ease. He could see a female constable waiting for him at the end of a track. He maneuvered the car off the main road. When he reached the constable, he let down the window and could see the tyre tracks of her squad car running up a narrow cul-de-sac. The lights ahead indicated a couple of dwellings.

The constable looked at his car doubtfully. 'I'd leave your car here, Inspector. Might get stuck up there. I'm Liv Fogelström. My partner Reuben Persson's up in the house with the family.' Hakim pressed the control and the window hissed back up. He got out. The snow had totally stopped.

'What have we got?'

They started crunching their way up the track. Hakim's suede shoes weren't exactly adequate footwear for the conditions, but he hadn't seen any forecasts for snow that morning. Surely in this day and age, the weather people could get something like that right!

'It's the father of the family. Tord Sundin. He's at the back of the house near the barn door, dressed in his Santa suit.'

The building immediately in front of Hakim – a typical, single-storey Scanian former farmhouse – was ablaze with lights. The road then curved round to the other dwelling, which was in semi-darkness. This appeared to be a more modern, two-storey building. Beyond, loomed the shadow of a coniferous wood.

'We'll see the victim first,' said Hakim, pulling his coat closer round him.

Hakim towered above Fogelström. He followed the constable, her pistol holster clamped to her side, past the front door and round the end of the first house. The building was L-shaped, with a large, detached barn some distance away and at right angles to the shorter leg of the L. The old farmyard was in the middle of the complex. Under the overhanging eaves of the house, where the snow hadn't fallen, Hakim could see it was now paved, and a few empty planters were dotted about. The outside lights at the back of the house were on, and near the threshold of the barn, Hakim could make out a red shape lying on the ground, half covered in snow. The body lay just in front of the structure's double doors, one of which was open; the prone figure preventing its closure. Hakim unconsciously held his breath, loath to break the eerie silence which follows a fresh snowfall. There were numerous footprints leading from the house and surrounding the victim. Fogelström read his mind.

'He died just before the snow started, apparently. So the prints are no indicators. They all came out to look.'

'Is there an obvious perpetrator? Someone who saw something?'

'Seems not. Sundin's wife looked out of the window to see where he was, as he was meant to be coming in a bit after four o'clock with the presents.' She indicated the barn with a jerk of her head. 'He'd gone in there to collect them and put on his costume. So, he must have been attacked on his way out.'

'And where are the presents?'

'Still in a sack, next to a freezer. Obviously came out without them.'

'Sure it was an attack?' Hakim said, slipping on his plastic gloves.

'It's pretty clear he was hit hard on the back of his head,' replied Fogelström. 'That makes it a suspicious death.' As Hakim crouched down, he could see that the head was covered by the red Santa hood. 'I put that back so you could see how he looked when we found him. But the elder son said his head was bare when he discovered the body. They covered it up so the younger son couldn't see.'

Hakim looked at the figure. From what he could make out, the victim was stocky and of medium height. When he slowly drew back the hood, he could see close-cropped hair, through which a large, unsightly lump on the back of the skull glared in bold relief.

'Any idea what was used to hit him, Inspector?'

Hakim glanced up. He shook his head. 'It must have been reasonably blunt. Certainly not something like a hammer, or anything spiked. There's not enough damage. Have you called forensics?'

'Em... no. We were waiting for you.'

'OK, Fogelström. Get straight onto them. Hopefully they'll have someone on duty.' He added to himself: 'If we're lucky, it'll be Eva Thulin.' Hakim took a glimpse at the barn's interior, which was poorly illuminated. 'Was this light on?' he called over his shoulder.

'Yes. When we got here. But apparently, it wasn't on when the body was found.'

Hakim wondered if Sundin himself had turned off the light before emerging from the barn. But if he had, why didn't he have the presents with him? Perhaps the killer had switched it off?

Fogelström disappeared round the corner so she could phone in from the squad car. Hakim straightened up and went into the barn. This part of the building was dimly lit by a single, high-hanging, naked bulb suspended from one of the rafters. It was used as a garage; the family Volvo sat comfortably in the space. An old motorbike was leaning against one wall, further along which was a shelf with a few tools on it. Judging by the pitch and angle of the roof, the barn had obviously been divided into two sections at some point in its history, and against the flimsily erected stud wall was a large chest freezer – there was the hessian sack containing the presents which *tomten* had failed to deliver. Next to the freezer was a doorway, which had evidently been recently widened; the right-hand section of the frame looked new, as did the door itself. Opposite the main entrance, just discernible in the furthest beam cast by the light, Hakim could make out another double door, which was closed. At least forensics could try and find something in here on the earth floor.

Fogelström was back. 'Forensics are on their way. Didn't sound too pleased.'

'Thanks. Well, we'd better see the family.'

The Sundin family were gathered in the living room. Six of them spread around. Two middle-aged women, a young man, two younger women, and a boy of about seven or eight who was trying to watch the television, which was playing quietly in the corner. Standing next to them was Fogelström's colleague. The brightly decorated Christmas tree made a mockery of the somber mood in the room. The fairy lights were on and some of the baubles were slowly rotating in the gentle thermals, winking at the white-faced assembly. Tinsel and paper chains, which had seen better days, were festooned around the walls, their ends tucked under pictures. Two candles, carved in the form of angels, were flickering on the window sill; and a large wooden reindeer, with a predominantly red nose, was nuzzling dangerously up to the open door of the log burner to keep warm.

'I'll speak to you all shortly. But, first, can I have a word with you, Constable?'

The constable followed Hakim out of the room into the hallway and closed the door behind him.

'OK, Persson, who's in there and what have you found out so far?'

Persson took out his notebook and glanced over his scribbles.

'The two older women. The thinner one is Tord Sundin's wife, Barbara. The other is the neighbour from the next-door house.' He scrutinized his notes. 'She's Felicia Thorsson. The Thorssons had come over to have a drink before the evening meal.'

'Thorssons? Is there a husband?'

'Yes. He's the one who rang in. The family were too shocked to react quickly. Well, that's what he said.'

'Where is he?'

'In the kitchen. Brewing up some coffee.'

'And the others?'

'Sundin's children. The eldest is his son, Mårten. Then his two daughters, Elvira and Susanne. The young kid is Georg.'

'And what are they saying happened?' Depending on Persson's answer, this was going to be an easy case to wrap up or become a potential nightmare.

'None of them know.' (Nightmare, thought Hakim.) 'Sundin went out to put on his Santa outfit, which was over in the barn. The presents were in a sack there too. When he didn't come back at four, Barbara Sundin sent Mårten out to look for him, who found him where he's lying.'

Hakim looked pensive. There wasn't going to be an easy solution; he would to have to interview all the members of the households individually to discover their alibis. Given the location of the two properties, the perpetrator was unlikely to have been conveniently passing at the exact time that Tord Sundin happened to be coming out of the barn. One thing Hakim was sure of – he needed help.

He went outside into the cold night air and called Anita on his mobile. The moment he clicked on her number and set the call in motion, he was having doubts. He knew he should be ringing Pontus Brodd. Anita might not take kindly to being dragged out on Christmas Eve and having to drive all the way over from Kristianstad in bad weather. Though it had stopped snowing here, it might be worse over on her side.

'Hello.'

'Hakim here.'

'Hi. Are you off duty now?' She didn't sound annoyed.

'No. Something's happened. A murder.'

'And you need help?' she said brightly, which took him aback.

'Well, yes. I know I should really phone Pontus–'

'Sod Brodd!'

He quickly filled her in on what he had found out, then gave her directions, as he knew Anita hadn't got round to getting a sat nav for her old car.

'Keep the family and neighbours apart, or make sure someone's watching them all the time,' was her parting piece of advice. 'I'll be across as soon as I can.'

CHAPTER 4

Another squad car had arrived at the same time as forensics technician, Eva Thulin, who was accompanied by a grouchy colleague. Hakim was pleased to see her, though she didn't seem overly ecstatic to be there and greeted him with a sarcastic 'Happy Christmas'. At least she might be able to give him a clue as to what was used to inflict the fatal blow. Another look round the barn hadn't enlightened him as to a possible instrument. Everything that could have been picked up and used had edges, which would have created more of a mess of Sundin's head.

He left Thulin and her partner setting up lights so that they could have a better view of the body. What he had to decide now was who should be interviewed first.

The headlights picked out the verges of the snow-covered road. On emerging from her aunt's house, the weather had taken Anita by surprise, and she had had to wipe a soft layer of snow from the windscreen of her car. Her old Peugeot wasn't the world's most reliable vehicle, though she was sure that the relatively new winter tyres would see her through to Malmö as long as there wasn't a further wintry blast. Her vision was temporarily impaired as her spectacles steamed up while she fought to get the car heater working. Her departure had been rapid and her excuses garbled. She could see the disapproval on her mother's face and the relief on her aunt's. Neither had made Anita particularly welcome, and the day had had none of the cheer that many Swedish households were enjoying at this festive time. The taboo subject, of course, was Lasse's Muslim girlfriend. Not only had Lasse not come over for Christmas, but he had taken an ethnic girl away on holiday with him to Tenerife – and goodness knows what they were getting up to there. Not that Anita's mother had actually said anything to Lasse – it was Anita who got it in the neck. It must have been her fault. It always was – it always had been. Why had her mother been so dissatisfied with her? Was it because Anita had been closer to her father? That was definitely seen as a betrayal after her parents' acrimonious divorce. And then Anita herself had divorced. According to her mother, she had never been good enough for Professor Björn Sundström, even when he became a serial adulterer. But charming Björn had always managed to get round his mother-in-law. No, Anita was a failure, both in her marriage and in the way she had brought up her son. One thing was certain: there was little Christmas spirit to be found in Kristianstad, not even the sort to be found in a bottle. She had half hoped that Kevin Ash, her quasi-long-distance boyfriend, would have invited her over to England for Christmas, but the invitation hadn't come. It wasn't exactly Kevin's fault – she knew that he was going over to see his daughters on Tyneside. With a malevolent ex-wife haunting proceedings, Anita's presence doubtless would have been an added inconvenience.

Hakim's phone call felt like a reprieve. The excuse she had prayed for. Not that someone being murdered was cause for celebration. But it got her away from the uncomfortable sofa bed, which always gave her backache, her aunt's awful meals, and another night sitting in silence with two bitter women – one because she had married and the other because she hadn't. She put on the radio and on came the station that played sixties music. That immediately lifted her mood and she concentrated hard on the road as she made her way out of Kristianstad and onto the E22. Another happy thought struck her – with Chief Inspector Moberg sweating his way round the bars of Tenerife, she and Hakim could investigate the murder without senior interference. Cracking it before he came back would give her immense satisfaction.

It was the distraught wife, Barbara Sundin, who sat on the edge of the single bed in front of Hakim in the small bedroom that he had purloined for the interviews. Barbara was a good one to start with. Maybe it was because he was used to working closely with Anita that he felt more comfortable dealing with a woman. And as the mother of the household, Barbara Sundin was probably better at giving him a more accurate timeline of the events that had taken place prior to the murder. Hakim reckoned that Barbara was slightly taller than her husband. She was slimmer, too, with frizzy blonde hair. Her face was fine-boned and would, without the tears that were blotching her mascara, be pretty. Hakim's immediate impression was that she wasn't a woman who normally wore much make-up, but had possibly made an effort for Christmas Eve.

'I'm sorry about this. It must be awful for you, but I need to ask questions now. The quicker I do, the quicker we can find out who attacked your husband. Are you OK with that?'

She wiped away a tear, a black stain running along her finger, then looked resolutely at Hakim.

'I know this might sound like an obvious question, but can you think of anybody who might have wanted to harm Tord?'

Barbara Sundin looked up, eyes opening wide as though she'd been startled. She shook her head. 'No. No. Besides, he was hardly ever here.'

'What do you mean?'

'Well, he travelled a lot.' This seemed to be the only explanation that she was going to offer.

'Sorry? Travelled a lot to where?' Hakim prompted.

Of course, she had to explain; this young policeman knew nothing of her husband. 'He was a chef. On ships.'

'Swedish ships?'

'No, all sorts of cargo ships. All over the world. He would jump onto a plane at Kastrup and meet up with a ship at some port. Usually he'd be away eight or nine weeks, and then fly back from wherever the ship docked. In fact, he wasn't due back in time for Christmas this year. It was all last minute.' She glanced across to the window. 'If he hadn't come back early then... this...' She began to sob softly again and Hakim waited for her to finish. While Barbara Sundin was composing herself, Hakim's mind began to whirl at the implications of what he had just been told.

'Can you go on?' he asked in as kindly a voice as he could muster, given that he was forcing back the impatience he was feeling.

'Yes. It's just...'

'I understand.'

She coughed and cleared her throat. 'We weren't expecting Tord until the New Year, so we weren't going to have a traditional Christmas. Mårten was going to go out in Malmö with his friends. Susanne wanted to be with her boyfriend. That seemed fine. Elvira, little Georg and I were going to have a quiet time.'

'But Tord came back and things changed?'

'Yes. We only had twenty-four hours' notice. His ship had docked in Shanghai a few days ahead of schedule.'

'And Tord liked a traditional Christmas? The tree, the food, *tomten*?'

Barbara Sundin nodded confirmation. 'Tord likes... liked his traditions. You probably don't do that sort of thing. Being... you know.'

He ignored her observation. 'So, you had to change things at the last minute?'

'Yes. It wasn't easy.' He could hear the panic in her voice.

'We were rushing around to get the right things in. Tord was very particular.'

'Would he have been upset if things weren't just right?'

'Ooh, yes. Everything had to be perfect.' Was that a hint of fear?

'Who did the cooking today?'

She seemed surprised. 'Oh, I see. Because he's a chef? No. He liked to be off duty when he came home. It was my job. But the girls helped. Well, Elvira did. Susanne isn't into cooking. Or helping. She's seventeen.' That was explanation enough.

'Your son Mårten is here, though. And Susanne. So, why they didn't go off and do what they had arranged?'

'Their father wouldn't have been happy. There would have been trouble. I didn't want that.'

Hakim was fast drawing his own conclusions as to the type of man Tord Sundin had been.

'Can I get you anything before we go on?'

She flashed him a grateful glance. 'I could do with some water.'

'No problem.' Hakim got up and went to the door. In the living room, the family and the two neighbours were gathered under the watchful eyes of Fogelström and Persson.

'Are we going to sit here all bloody night?' Mårten Sundin said, getting to his feet. He didn't hide his contempt for the foreign-looking inspector.

'You'll stay here for as long as it takes,' Hakim answered firmly. 'Persson, can you take a glass of water into fru Sundin? Thanks.'

Mårten Sundin sank back onto the sofa next to his sister Elvira. He was still muttering when Hakim left the room and went outside. Under the arc lights, he could see Eva Thulin in her white overalls chatting to her colleague, who had just been taking photos under her directions.

'Cracked the case already before Anita gets here?' Thulin

said with a wry grin. Her mood had improved.

'No such luck. Any joy here?'

'Well, cracked is the word. This man was bashed on the head. One blow. Definitely murder.'

'Weapon?'

She shrugged. 'To be honest, I'm at a loss at the moment. It wasn't anything sharp. Nor anything like a hammer. I can't think what was used. It might be round or curved... but heavy and firm; certainly, fatal. There's a small imprint on the skin which I can't work out at the moment. I'll get a closer look back at the lab.'

'Time of death?'

'Between three and four; nearer four, I suspect.'

'That ties in with what the family reported.'

Hakim was about to head back into the house.

'Can't tell whether he was actually killed out here or was attacked just inside the barn and staggered out. There are some obvious scuff marks on the earth floor just inside the door, but nothing that is easily identifiable and nothing that indicates a specific sequence of events. But I don't think the victim was expecting to be attacked; there are no defence wounds.'

Hakim idly kicked away some snow. 'That makes sense. He knew the perpetrator.' He jerked a thumb over his shoulder. 'It's one of that lot in there.'

CHAPTER 5

'Tord arrived last night. Elvira picked him up from the station.'

'And you managed to get everything organized by then?'

Barbara Sundin gave a wan smile. 'Just about.'

'OK,' Hakim continued as he watched Sundin's wife hunched over her glass of water, holding it tightly as though it was a crutch that kept her supported. Was she the broken woman he had first assumed? Or was it a relief that her controlling husband was gone? It hadn't taken much to read between the lines. Would it be confirmed by the rest of the family? 'Today. Christmas Eve. How did it pan out?'

She gave him a fleeting look of surprise. 'Just like a normal Christmas Eve.' This was followed by an embarrassed pause. 'Well, our sort of Christmas. I don't expect you... Well, you know what I mean.'

'Please, just go through the day.'

'We exchanged one or two presents in the morning, but the main ones were to be brought in by *tomten*. By, you know...'

'Your husband.'

She nodded slowly. When she spoke again, her voice was thick with emotion, though she was describing a simple process. She had been in the kitchen most of the day. She, with Elvira's help, had made the *lutefisk* with mashed potatoes and mustard sauce, followed by *risgrynsgröt*, a white rice porridge. Hakim

21

had never had *lutefisk*, but had heard that it was disgusting. It was dried cod or ling that had then been soaked in lye for several days so it bloats. Then it's steamed before serving and, according to Anita, who had to endure the dish at her aunt's, it ends up with a gelatinous texture and tastes like blubber. She said that the only way to eat it was with swift shots of *besk*, a lethal alcoholic herbal schnapps popular in Skåne that does wonders for stripping the lining from one's throat. Hakim could never quite get his head round some of the weird eating traditions of his country. *Surströmming* – "smelly fish" (fermented Baltic herring) eaten in late summer – was another one.

After washing up, she had gone on to prepare for the evening meal of meatballs and smoked ham, sill and salmon. It appeared that the woman had spent most of her festive day chained to the cooker and the sink.

'I know you seem to have been in the kitchen a lot of the day, but were you aware of any ill feeling among the family? Tensions?'

'No, why would there be?'

'Well, Mårten and Susanne had planned to do other things. Weren't they annoyed?'

She waved that away with a dismissive hand gesture. 'There are always little arguments. All families are the same. I'm sure yours is no different. Elvira didn't want to spend so much time with me in the kitchen. But it's only for a day.'

'And what did Tord do all day?'

'He was tired. So he relaxed. Watched the telly. Had a few drinks.' In response to Hakim's quizzical expression, she quickly put in: 'He deserved to rest. He had been away for weeks, and then a long flight.'

'One last thing. We think Tord was probably attacked some time before four. Where were you then?'

She seemed to crumple again. 'In the kitchen, I suppose.'

'And Elvira was with you?'

'She was earlier, and then she went to change for the evening meal. But I kept popping back into the living room to see how Georg was. Felicia was with him some of the time. Tord was there before he must have gone out to prepare. Georg was watching *Kalle Anke och hans vänner*. He loves the Disney hour. And he was getting so excited that *tomten* would come in soon after the programme finished. Of course, he knew it would be his dad, but the thought of lots of presents... you know.'

'How old is Georg?'

'He just turned eight in November.' She couldn't hide the pride in her voice. Obviously a late addition to the Sundin family, and Mamma's favourite, by the sound of it.

'So, who was it who actually found the body?'

'Mårten. I sent him out to find his dad. I wondered why he had been so long.'

'Did you see any of the others around during that time?'

'Why are you asking?' she said in sudden alarm. 'For goodness' sake, I hope you don't suspect any of the family had anything to do with this. That's an awful thing to think, Inspector.'

Mårten was just as surly as he had been from the moment Hakim had stepped into the house. He had blond, tightly curled hair like his mother and wore a short-sleeved, black T-shirt that enabled him to show off his tattoos. The designs showed interlaced fabulous creatures writhing from shoulder to wrist on both arms. The artistry was impressive – they wouldn't have been cheap to get done. His low-slung khaki trousers constantly appeared to be about to drop off his backside, disconcertingly revealing his black underpants. Hakim wished he would sit down.

'I hope you didn't give Mamma a hard time. Can't you see she's upset?' His tone was as aggressive as his body language as he hovered on the opposite side of the bed. In the "interview room", the clothes still strewn on the floor and a lack of anything on the walls showed that this wasn't a bedroom that was used very often. Barbara Sundin had apologized for the mess, but Elvira was sleeping in here. She had explained that her elder daughter didn't come home that often – she was in her last year at university in Gothenburg and usually stayed up there with her friends during the holidays. This had been her first visit back since August.

'Apparently, you found the body.'

The aggression suddenly subsided. 'I'm just glad Mamma didn't discover him.'

'She sent you to find him?'

'Yeah. She wondered where he'd got to. He went over to the barn to put on his Santa gear. Bloody stupid tradition, but Georg was excited. Mamma didn't want him to be disappointed.' He sighed. 'She dotes on him.'

'So you went to look for your dad?'

'I thought he was just pissing us off as usual. Keeping us waiting.'

'Was that typical?'

'Oh, yeah. Whenever he came back, he expected the family to jump. We always had to do what he wanted. Like this fucking Christmas shit. It's just to please him. None of the rest of us would be bothered. Except Georg, of course.'

'The body?'

'I found him lying in the snow. At first I thought he was drunk and had just fallen over.'

'Had he been drinking a lot?'

'He always did when he was at home. While Mamma was slaving away in the kitchen, he was swigging back the booze.' Hakim made a quick note on his pad.

'Then you realized that something more serious had happened?'

'Well, obviously,' he said sarcastically. 'He didn't move. He had no pulse. And he had a bloody great lump on the back of his head.'

'Did you see anybody else outside when you found the body?'

'No.'

'And where were you between three and four this afternoon?'

'In my room. I wanted to get away from all the rubbish. I had my music on. I was sick of all that Christmas jingly crap that Dad liked.'

'So you didn't hear anything? Noise of a struggle?'

He shook his head. 'The music,' was all he would say by way of explanation.

'I hear you'd planned to go out with your friends,' said Hakim, taking a different tack.

'That's right. Some of the lads from the docks.'

'The docks?'

'Yeah, I work there. Drive forklift trucks.'

'So, what were you and the lads going to do?'

'Bumming round Malmö. Have a few drinks, a few laughs.'

'And why didn't you?'

'Dad.'

'You're old enough to do your own thing,' Hakim observed.

Mårten gave a mirthless laugh. 'It wouldn't be worth the hassle. More arguments with the old man. If I hadn't been here, he'd have taken it out on Mamma. He usually did. Always finding fault.'

'Did you have an argument over going out this time?'

He looked evasive. 'Not really.'

'So something was said?'

'It was something or nothing. We didn't get along, but I didn't want to spoil the day for the others.'

'OK; that's all for the moment.'

Mårten wandered over to the door, hitching up his trousers, which immediately slipped back down.

'Oh, by the way, why were Arne and Felicia Thorsson here?'

'They're our neighbours.'

'I know. But this was your family day.'

'They haven't got kids. Mamma had asked them over before she knew that Dad was coming home early. They're good to her when he's away.'

Hakim tapped the end of his notebook against his chin.

'What did your dad make of them coming round?'

'He didn't mind.'

The remark produced a doubtful look from Hakim. 'From what I've heard so far, your father doesn't strike me as a man who would want his traditional family Christmas disturbed by others.'

Mårten suddenly smirked. 'Have you seen Felicia's tits?'

CHAPTER 6

The first thing Elvira Sundin did when she came into the bedroom to be interviewed by Inspector Mirza was tidy up her clothes. 'Mamma told me to. She's house-proud.'

Hakim let her finish before he started to question her. He peeked at his watch and wondered how long Anita was going to be. There were still three other people to talk to – he wasn't going to bother with Georg, whom his mother had taken off to watch television before putting him to bed. This was one Christmas that the little boy would never forget; jolted out of his childhood innocence by a brutal blow to his father's head. Could he ever look at *tomten* again?

'When did you come down from Gothenburg?'

Elvira was tall and blonde; her wavy hair reached her shoulders. But she was no classical Nordic beauty; her features were square and almost masculine. There was no sign of make-up, though she was wearing a short, brightly coloured dress, which confirmed what her mother had said about her going to change for the evening meal.

'Three days ago.'

'When you came down, I assume you didn't know then that your father would be home for Christmas.'

She crossed her legs as she sat on the corner of the bed. She shook her head.

27

'Would you have come home if you had known he was coming?'

She was obviously surprised by the question, and she hesitated before she answered. 'Yes.'

'You don't sound sure.'

'I promised to help Mamma. I knew the Thorssons were coming from next door. And I wanted to see Georg opening his presents.' She gave a kind of snort. 'Poor kid; more than one thing has died tonight.' She picked at the edge of the duvet.

'Tell me about the presents.'

'I sorted them out last night and put them in a sack. Susanne put them in the barn so Georg wouldn't find them. And she looked out the Santa suit when we knew *he'd* be coming back. Mamma knew he would insist on doing his *tomten* thing.'

'What was the general atmosphere like today? With your father around, I mean.'

She stared at Hakim. 'Do you get shit from your colleagues? For being an immigrant? You don't see many dark faces among cops.'

'I'm not an immigrant. My parents are,' he added defensively, temporarily taken off guard by her question.

'Does your presence cause tension? Make other cops uneasy?'

'Why are you asking?'

'Dad. When he came back into the family, everybody became tense. He made us uneasy. He played games with us.'

'Games?' Hakim queried.

'Mind games. Playing one off against the other. Upsetting one, praising another, then vice versa. And all the time being mean to Mamma.' She now began to twiddle with a large amber ring. 'To answer your question, everything was jovial on the surface, but underneath...'

Hakim scribbled some more notes. 'You don't happen to study psychology by any chance?' This was accompanied by a grin.

Elvira smiled back. 'It's one of my modules.'

'Were there any specific arguments?'

'Do you suspect one of us?' It appeared as though the thought hadn't crossed her mind before.

'We're not jumping to conclusions. Anyhow, Elvira, were there any arguments involving your father today?'

'Just the usual. Dad and Mårten had a bit of a row this morning.'

'About what?'

'I think it was something about him going out for a while to see his mates. Dad was adamant that he stay here with the family. Nothing really serious.' Again, the ring was twisted a complete turn round her finger. 'Susanne was unhappy with him. She should have been with her boyfriend today. She shouted at him and stormed off for a while.'

'And what was that about?'

'You're better off asking her.'

'OK, when was that?'

She puffed out her lips. 'This morning some time. I was in the kitchen and heard raised voices outside in the yard. But Susanne's huffy these days. I just avoid getting involved.'

There was a knock on the door.

'Come,' Hakim called.

Liv Fogelström popped her head round. 'Inspector Sundström's arrived. Thought you'd like to know.'

'Thanks. I'll be right out.' The door closed again. Hakim snapped his notebook shut. 'Just one other thing: where were you between three and four this afternoon?'

'You want an alibi?' Her eyes opened wide in mock incredulity. 'Well, I was in the kitchen a lot of the time helping my stressed mamma. Then I came in here to change. I thought I should make an effort. And I didn't want to sit in the living room making small talk with Felicia.'

'How long have you known the Thorssons?'

'Ages. Well, Arne. He moved in next door when I was quite young. Like an uncle to us really. He's lovely.'

'And his wife?'

'He only married Felicia about five years ago.' Was that disapproval written across her face? Hakim quickly followed this up.

'I gather that she's not one of your favourite people if you wanted to avoid her.'

'Never thought Arne would marry. Confirmed bachelor. Then he goes off on holiday to Thailand one Christmas and the next thing we know, he's got Felicia in tow.'

'Don't you approve?'

'Arne seems happy enough. She's into expensive things, which is not really his scene. Though he has money. I suppose she's a natural flirt. She makes sure men notice her.'

'Did your father?'

'I suppose,' came the cautious answer.

Hakim found Anita rooting around in the barn. A broad grin greeted him. She didn't have to explain – he had provided her with an escape route from Kristianstad.

'Trying to find the weapon?'

Anita lightly tapped the bottom of her glasses with the end of her thumb as though pushing them back up her nose. 'Hmmm. Eva filled me in. Oh, I hope you don't mind, but I said she could take the body away.' She looked reflective: there had been something about the body that she couldn't quite put her finger on.

Hakim shrugged. 'You're now the senior officer on the crime scene.' It was said without any rancour. In fact, he was relieved that Anita was here now. Not that he felt he couldn't cope, but with so many suspects in one place, it was easier to split the interviewing duties.

Anita scanned the space like a hawk looking for voles.

She had tried the car doors; they were locked. Scrutiny of the tool shelf had revealed an assortment of innocuous motoring equipment: jump leads, a couple of small spanners, a crumpled oil rag, an ancient foot pump, a plastic oil bottle and an old windscreen wiper whose rubber blade had come loose. Below the shelf were a couple of jerry cans. They were virtually empty. She had tried them for weight already. There was nothing obvious that could have inflicted the fatal wound.

'Is that significant?' she said, nodding towards the inner door.

'Don't think so. Thulin found the key for it on Sundin's body; it was part of a bunch – all the barn keys on the same ring. In fact, he was lying on them, so his assailant couldn't have got the murder weapon from in there. We found it locked. One of the constables and I had a quick look inside after talking to Thulin; it seemed to have a lot of old junk in it. Usual sort of storage. Locked, I think, because there's also a smart ride-on mower in there – probably why the door was widened – and some gardening equipment: they must have quite a spread out there. No, I think our killer has got rid of whatever it was that he or she used. Or hidden it; though, admittedly, they wouldn't have had much time to do so.'

'Well, you'd better tell me what you've found out now that you've had time to talk to some of the people in the house,' Anita said absently as she lifted up the lid of the chest freezer. 'Needs a thorough defrost, this. That's some build-up of ice. Even worse than mine. But my excuse is that I don't use it much since Lasse moved out. Sorry,' she apologized and let the freezer lid drop back into place.

'I've talked to Sundin's wife, elder son, Mårten, and Elvira, the older of the two sisters.'

'And?' By this time they had wandered to the entrance of the barn. The snow was beginning to freeze and gleamed with an argentine sheen in the lights.

'The wife seemed suitably upset, though I got the impression that she might've been slightly afraid of her husband. That was as good as confirmed by the other two. Neither Mårten nor Elvira seemed distraught by his death. I get the impression that they thought he was a bully who didn't treat their mother well.'

'Potential suspects?'

'Possibly. Protecting their mother? He'd been drinking. It'll be interesting to find out how much alcohol he had in him when he was attacked. Enough to set off an argument, and too much to defend himself?'

Anita could see her breath as she asked: 'Are we looking at someone who's in there at the moment? Or is this something else entirely?'

Hakim shook his head confidently. 'No. I'm fairly sure it's tied up with the family or the neighbours. It's not just the fact that these are the only two houses around here, but no one knew Sundin was going to be back for Christmas. Not even his family.'

'Oh?' Anita sounded surprised.

'Sundin worked as a chef on big ocean-going cargo ships: a couple of months on, a month off type of thing. He wasn't due back until New Year. His ship got into Shanghai early and he jumped on a plane. Panic here to get everything ready for the traditional Christmas that he always insisted on. Put some of the family's noses out of joint because they had already made plans. But what Tord wants, Tord gets – and sod everybody else. That's my reading of the situation anyway. So, one thing we know for sure is that this murder wasn't planned.'

CHAPTER 7

The Thorssons' living room was more sophisticated than the Sundin household's next door. They didn't have kids for a start. The furniture was a strange mix of the plain and the extravagant. It was a clash of styles and tastes. From what Hakim had gleaned, Arne Thorsson had married late and his sparse home had been invaded by the younger, more flamboyant Felicia. Certain things had been left as they were, like Arne's old wooden chair, in which he was now sitting, but the rest of the seating was richly adorned in flouncy chintz. The obligatory ship on the window sill had been allowed to stay, but other surfaces had been swallowed up by Felicia's knick-knacks. As though to continue the pattern, Arne was dressed in sensible, muted trousers, shirt and jersey, while Felicia wore a short, bright red-and-yellow dress with a revealing cleavage. Her strawberry-blonde hair cascaded down to her shoulders and framed a face that was sharpened by excessive make-up. Anita thought that all that effort hadn't really made her any more attractive, as she wasn't particularly eye-catching in the first place. However, what she did have was a sensual body that her dress did nothing to disguise. And, as Mårten had pointed out to Hakim, her breasts were her most dominant feature. A similar age to Anita, Felicia had the confidence in her appearance that she herself had never possessed. Maybe that's why Anita took an instant dislike to her and why she deliberately kept her waiting while she interviewed her husband first.

Anita had agreed with Hakim that he should finish talking to the family – there was only Susanne left – while she tackled the Thorssons ('I'd better take the voluptuous Felicia or she might have you for breakfast.'). Then they would compare notes. As Anita expected that no one was going to hold their hands up for the crime, they were going to have to find the culprit through evidence. But at least they could establish who had a possible motive first.

When she asked her first question, she noticed that Arne was avoiding eye contact.

'How long have you known Tord Sundin?'

'It's dreadful, isn't it? How could this happen? Here! Dreadful!' He shook his head in disbelief as he contemplated his constantly wriggling, interwoven fingers.

'Yes. Dreadful indeed. But can you tell me how long you've known Tord?'

'A long time. I don't know. Ever since I moved here.' He seemed to be trying to find the answer in his hands. Then he looked up. 'Seventeen years.'

'And you've always got on with the Sundin family?'

'Of course,' he said tentatively as though he was answering a trick question. 'I've watched the kids grow up.'

Anita's eye caught sight of a wooden duck dressed in tartan in a cabinet behind Thorsson's chair. What was that all about?

'And what was Tord like?'

'What do you mean?' His gaze had dropped to his lap again.

'Was he a nice guy? Was he a helpful neighbour?'

'He wasn't around that much.' The answer was evasive. 'He was often away at sea. All over the world.'

'Did you help him out?'

'Not really. But I did come round and help Barbara sometimes. When he was away. Like when her boiler broke down a couple of winters ago. And I sometimes chopped wood for her. Only small things. Just kept an eye.'

'You were always there for her?'

'I like to think so.' He lowered his voice as though Felicia might be listening at the door. 'Barbara's a nice lady.'

'I'm sure she appreciated your efforts.' Was he more than a good neighbour? The thought flitted across Anita's mind. 'But I need to get to know Tord a bit more. I don't know... was he the sort of person you'd have a drink with, or go fishing with... whatever?'

'We had some this afternoon. Drink that is.' He raised his eyes again and shot Anita a worried look. 'He'd had quite a lot by the time we arrived.'

'Was he drunk?'

'No. Nothing like that. But he could...' Arne's voiced trailed off.

'He could what?' Anita asked sharply.

'He could get... well, not exactly nasty but... what's the word?' He frowned for a moment. 'Confrontational. That's what I would call it.'

'And who was he being confrontational with today?'

'Mårten for one. And I believe he'd had an argument with Susanne.'

'What about?'

'Her boyfriend, I think.'

Anita hoped that Hakim was getting to the bottom of that. 'And what about you?'

His face creased in puzzlement. 'I don't understand.'

'Was he confrontational with you?'

'Not really.'

Anita could tell that something was niggling at him. 'Did he say something to upset you? The drink talking? People come out with stuff they don't always mean, but it can still be hurtful.' She could see that she had stumbled across a point of conflict.

Whether he would say anything was another matter.

'It was nothing.'

'It must have been something,' Anita pushed.

Arne Thorsson appeared to be a cautious man, and like many Swedish males, not comfortable when discussing personal subjects. 'It was silly. I shouldn't have let myself get annoyed.' But annoyed he had been, judging by the hint of bitterness in his voice. Anita said nothing, but gave him an encouraging smile. 'He just said something inappropriate. I'm sure he meant it as a joke.'

'Jokes can be spiteful.'

'I didn't like it. He made some remark about my wife's... you know.' He waved his hand in front of his chest. 'It's not the sort of thing you should say in front of a woman; certainly not before the woman's husband.'

'And was your wife upset?'

His eyes blazed for a second before he managed to control his rising ire. 'She just laughed it off. But she's good at handling these situations.' But you're not, thought Anita. A naïve, reserved man in late middle age marrying a brassy, younger woman who courted attention – could it drive such a man to murder?

'So, can you take me through your movements today?' He gave her a questioning look: 'I just need to establish a timeline leading up to Tord's death. What was happening before and where everybody was.'

'You can't think–' he began to protest.

'I don't think anything yet. I have to establish all the facts first. So, take me though your day up until the police arrived.'

He cleared his throat before he began. He might appear an unassuming and gentle man, but he was certainly physically up to braining someone. The hand he raised to cover his mouth was large and rough; he was obviously used to manual work. Whether a cruel or just plain stupid remark about his wife's large bosom was enough to tip him over the edge was something else.

Anita berated herself for thinking too far ahead.

'We had a quiet morning. Exchanged our gifts. Felicia made us an early lunch. She doesn't go in for all that *lutefisk*. Afterwards, we went for a short walk in the wood behind here to work off our meal, as we knew we'd be having another one at six with Barbara and the family. Got some fresh air before going over to the Sundins' place at about a quarter past two. We had some drinks. Then we watched a bit of that Disney programme on the television with Georg. At some stage Tord must have gone off to change into his *tomten* costume in the barn.'

'Sorry, let's go back. Presumably, it was before he went out to the barn that he'd come out with the off-colour joke about your wife?'

Arne moved uneasily in his seat. 'Yes.'

'So, what did everybody do after he went out?'

'I don't know. I'd gone out myself by then. But I think Barbara and Elvira were in the kitchen taking care of the evening meal. Mårten and Susanne had made themselves scarce.'

'And you and Felicia?'

He frowned. 'We sat with Georg for a few minutes and then I went out as soon as I saw Tord pouring himself another drink.'

'Where did you go?'

'I just went for a wander. I had to get out.'

'Was that because you were upset about Tord's remark?'

Again, he coughed. 'You could say that. It just created a bad atmosphere. Not that it was that good when we arrived. I got the impression that the lunch had been quite tense. Not a lot of seasonal goodwill.'

'Did your wife go with you?' He shook his head. 'And how long were you out?'

'Half an hour. Perhaps a bit longer. I was heading back to the Sundins' when I heard Mårten shouting. I came running into the yard, and there was Mårten by the barn door, bending over what turned out to be Tord's body. Elvira and Susanne arrived soon after.'

'What was Mårten shouting? Could you hear?'

'Yes. He was shouting at his mother to take Georg back into the house so that he couldn't see his dad.'

Anita paused for a few seconds as she mentally processed this information. 'I believe it was you who rang the police?'

'I did. Once we realized that Tord was dead, the rest of the family were too shocked to react. I took it upon myself to phone.'

'And until the police arrived, what was everybody doing?'

'We were all in the house. Felicia was comforting Barbara in the kitchen. Elvira was doing her best to distract Georg. He hadn't actually seen the body and he was wondering why *tomten* hadn't turned up. It was all so terrible.'

Anita pursed her lips. 'Are you sure that no one saw you when you went for your "wander"?'

His gaze drifted towards the window and the sailing boat. 'No.' Then his head swivelled back and, for the first time, his eyes fixed upon hers. 'I had nothing to do with Tord's death. Absolutely nothing.'

Susanne was a sullen teenager. That was Hakim's immediate impression. Like Elvira, she was tall. But, unlike her sister, she was striking. Her blonde hair was cut in an urchin style, which accentuated her height. She wore what looked like new jeans and a grey, knitted jersey which had a white Nordic pattern weaving its way across the front, back and upper arms. It looked brand new and wasn't the sort of garment that Susanne seemed comfortable wearing. She fiddled with one sleeve distractedly as she saw Hakim staring at her.

'Nice jersey.' He tried to break the ice.

She scowled. 'Mamma knitted it. Wanted me to wear something smart for Christmas.' She spat out the word "smart" as though it was some sort of disease.

'I'm sorry about your father and that I have to talk to you about it.'

'You're doing your job.' He was surprised that she had responded so positively before he had even asked his first question.

'That's right. I'm doing my job. So, I have to ask you why you had an argument with your dad today.'

'How do you know that?' she said fiercely. 'I know; fucking Elvira! She can be a real cow sometimes. Thinks she's too good for us these days; up there in Gothenburg with her snooty uni friends.' This was far from the monosyllabic teenager he'd been expecting, but it was tempered by a lot of anger. She had wide-open blue eyes that were simultaneously arresting and unfathomable.

'The argument? You shouted at your dad.'

'He pissed me off.'

Hakim waited for her to elaborate. Nothing was forthcoming. 'Why had he pissed you off?'

Susanne eventually said with some reluctance. 'Lucas.'

'Lucas? Who's he?'

She pulled at the collar of the jumper as if it were chafing her neck. 'My boyfriend.'

'And you were originally meant to be having Christmas with him?' All she did was purse her lips grumpily. She seemed to have gone into her shell. 'Were you arguing about not going to his place for Christmas?'

'Sort of.'

'Sort of? Was there anything else?'

She looked at Hakim defiantly. 'Dad didn't like Lucas.' There was no disguising the fury in her tone. 'He said some nasty things about him. I wasn't having that. He disappears for months on end then comes back here and tells everybody what they should do.' It all came flooding out. 'How dare he tell me who I should be going out with! He's only met Lucas twice. It's *my* life!'

Hakim let her calm down before quietly asking: 'When and where did you have this row?'

She cocked her head and gave him a lopsided glance. 'This morning.'

'Where?'

'Outside the kitchen. I was having a smoke.'

'Did he disapprove of that? The smoking, I mean.'

'No.' Her faced brightened. 'He smoked himself so he could hardly point a finger. But the thought of his daughter shagging someone he didn't like; that wasn't on.' Hakim was given a jolt by her frankness. Susanne immediately picked up on his awkwardness. 'You're quite cute when you're embarrassed.' For some reason Hakim found himself rather pleased at being described as "cute", particularly by a good-looking girl. It threw him and he stuttered before he could ask her where she was when her father was attacked.

'I'd gone for a walk. Then it started to snow.'

'You don't strike me as the outdoor sort.'

That fierce glare was there again. 'You have no idea what "sort" I am. I *needed* to get out of the house.' Again, she showed no inclination to elaborate.

'Why did you need to get out of the house?'

She gave him a pitying look. 'Why do you think? It was crap. No one was happy, except Dad. He was drunk and horrible. And that tart from next door had come round.'

'Felicia Thorsson?'

'*Her*,' she said with undisguised loathing.

'So where did you go for your walk?'

Susanne jerked her head towards the door. 'The wood at the back. I often go there.' She grinned as though some wicked thought had struck her. 'That's where I first *did it* with Lucas.'

But Hakim wasn't going to take the rise this time. 'How long were you out?'

'I dunno. I phoned Lucas when I was out. I needed to talk to someone normal.'

'So how long did you speak to him for?'

'Quite a long time,' she said offhandedly. 'I had a lot to unload on him. All the shit here. He's a good listener.'

'When did you get back from your walk?'

'When I heard some shouts from the yard. Came back and found Arne and Mårten leaning over Dad. He was in that silly Santa suit.'

One last question: 'On your way back from the wood, you didn't see anyone else around; near the house, or the Thorssons' place? Or anything suspicious?'

At first, she seemed puzzled by the suggestion. Then she said slowly, 'Now I think about it, there *was* something. A noise. A shape possibly. At the side of the house.' She wrinkled her nose. 'Didn't think about it at the time because of the shouting. It could have been an animal. But it could have been someone.'

CHAPTER 8

Felicia Thorsson appeared to be out of sorts. The clothes were immaculate, as were her hair and make-up, but something was amiss. The fact that her neighbour had just been murdered would, of course, explain it, but Anita thought it would be interesting to find out if there was anything more. Felicia sat on the plush sofa cradling a tumbler of a clear liquid. Judging by the lack of sparkle, Anita reckoned the gin in the glass was swamping any tonic that had been added to the mix. Felicia appeared to be in need of it and had obviously had a few before the interview started.

'You look upset.'

'Wouldn't you be?' The retort wasn't angry. Sad, if anything.

'I understand it must be distressing. Especially on such a day as this.' Empathy was the route Anita was taking and it seemed to work, as Felicia managed a faint smile.

Felicia Thorsson described her day. It matched that of her husband's, though he hadn't gone into how long she had taken to doll herself up for their visit to the Sundins.

'And what was Tord like when you got over there?'

'Oh, Tord was Tord. He'd had a bit too much of this,' she said holding up her glass. 'I think he'd upset some of the family. They weren't expecting him, you know. All very last minute. Poor Barbara was all of a dither. I offered to help.' She slurped some more of her drink. 'But she said she could cope. She's a Trojan, that one.'

'Do you know how he had upset the family?'

Felicia gave a low cackle. 'Oh, he was a wind-up merchant. Very good at needling people. But it was just his way. Liked to get a reaction. No wonder, after being stuck on bloody ships for weeks on end with all those Chinese or Vietnamese seamen, or whatever they are, who didn't speak Swedish.' Then she thought about it for a moment. 'English, anyway. Not much fun. He liked a bit of fun.'

'I hear he made an off-colour remark about you.'

She glanced provocatively down at her cleavage. 'He made a joke about these. But he always did that. It upset Arne, but,' she said confidentially, 'he's a bit old-fashioned about things like that. Don't get me wrong; Arne's a marvellous man. But it's nice for a woman to have her attributes appreciated. You're nice looking. You know what I mean.'

Anita wasn't going to get drawn into a debate on the point.

'But you were OK with it?'

'Of course I was. Tord was always like that with me. Playful. That's the word. Playful with me, anyway.'

'Anything more?' Anita slipped the question in as Felicia was taking another gulp.

After she came up for air, she shook her head vigorously. 'Of course not! I'm a married woman,' she bridled.

'But he fancied you?'

She now became misty-eyed. 'Once, maybe.' There was a hint of a tear, which she dabbed away with her free hand. 'You know what men are like.'

'If Tord didn't chase you, did he go after other women?'

'How should I know? You'd have to ask Barbara.'

Anita doubted that would be a very productive conversation. Did Tord mean more to Felicia than she was letting on?

'I know this is sensitive, but could Arne have been jealous

of Tord's attentions to you? That maybe he mistakenly thought there was more going on between you two than there actually was?'

Felicia was so taken aback by the suggestion that she nearly spilt her drink. 'Goodness me, no! Nothing went on. Nothing for him to be jealous about. Just silly remarks. That's all.' Then she knocked back what was left in her glass and looked round for a refill.

Anita asked her final question: 'Where were you between three and four today?'

'I stayed most of the time watching that *Donald Duck* programme with Georg. You know, the one they put on every Christmas. The little mite was getting so excited that *tomten* was coming. Didn't know it was his dad, of course.' Then her forehead creased in thought. 'Or maybe he did, but didn't want to let that spoil the moment the presents arrived.'

'And you were there all the time?'

'Em... Arne had gone out. Actually, I popped back here just to get a quick...' she shook the glass in her hand. 'They didn't have any gin over there. It's my tipple. But I wasn't long.' So she probably wasn't in the house when Tord was killed. Despite the drink, Felicia seemed to be reading Anita's thoughts. 'But I was back in their living room when all the commotion took place outside,' she added hurriedly.

Anita met up with Hakim outside the barn. Tord Sundin's body had been removed and only the police tape round the crime scene was left. They wanted to talk away from the family and neighbours. As Anita adjusted to the arctic conditions, she stamped her feet and suddenly had the urge for a cigarette. Or at least some snus. Sometimes giving up tobacco seemed a sacrifice too far.

'How did you get on?' Hakim asked as he blew into his cupped hands to try and keep them warm.

'I get the impression that Arne Thorsson disliked Sundin. And Felicia liked him too much.'

'There's not much weeping going on in there,' Hakim said, gesturing towards the main house. 'Susanne didn't seem to like her father any more than Mårten or Elvira. The only one who appears to be genuinely upset is his wife. And Georg, of course.'

'So, in theory, all of them could be suspects.'

'Certainly the three older children. And the Thorssons?'

Anita had managed to conquer her tobacco craving. 'Arne, yes. Don't know about Felicia. I'd like to know whether there was more to her flirtatious relationship with Sundin. If there was, then Arne would have a strong motive.' She stamped her feet again to try and keep the circulation going. 'There's nothing more we can do here at the moment. We'll leave one of the constables overnight in case one of our suspects tries to do a bunk. It'll also make the killer uneasy to have a police presence. And then why don't you come back to my place and we'll have something to eat? Unless you're due to be with your parents?'

'No, that's fine. I had nothing planned. We're not Christmas people.'

'OK, I'll have a word with them all before we leave and explain the situation.' She grimaced. 'You're right; one of them did it.'

Hakim coughed. 'Well, I might not be.'

'What do you mean?'

'Well, according to Susanne, there might have been someone snooping around about the time of the murder.'

'I don't believe it!'

CHAPTER 9

They drove back to the centre of Malmö so Hakim could drop off the pool car at the polishus. As Anita headed towards her apartment, it occurred to her that she hadn't really got anything in the house to eat. Pizzas in the freezer, but she hadn't stocked up with much else, as she had expected to spend the next few days with her mother. Fortunately, there were still eating places open around Möllevångstorget, and she stopped off at a Thai restaurant she sometimes went to and got a carry-out. Not exactly festive, but she was now starving. Along with a half-drunk bottle of red still hanging around in the kitchen – Hakim had juice – they sat down for their very late Christmas dinner. Anita couldn't remember enjoying one more. She raised her glass of wine: '*God Jul!*'

Hakim smiled back, a forkful of food hovering close to his mouth. 'Sorry to drag you away from your mother's.'

Anita took a sip and raised her glass again. 'That's worth a second toast. My aunt's a shocking cook. Surprised my mother's still alive.'

Hakim laughed, despite never being quite sure whether Anita was joking or not. They didn't discuss the case until they had finished eating and had moved into the living room. What would he be doing now if he wasn't with Anita? Probably sitting at home by himself watching some daft telly programme; or doing the same thing round at his parents' place, watching a similarly daft telly programme from a Middle Eastern station. Relaxing with Anita was far more preferable – and he was finding that he was getting increasingly excited about the case. He really was on the front line with this one. No Moberg, no Brodd, no interference.

It was past midnight when they briefly summed up their thoughts.

'As far as I can ascertain,' said Hakim, kicking off, 'Tord left the house at roughly a quarter past three to go to the barn to put on his costume and pick up the presents. He probably also went to sober up a bit – they all indicated that he had been drinking most of the day. He certainly had time to kill, if you'll excuse the pun, before coming back at four after the Disney programme had finished to do his *tomten* act. Or he may have left the house early to talk to someone specifically – a prearranged meet. Whatever the reason was, he unlocked the main barn door – Persson got that from one of the family who said he was very particular about keeping it locked: extremely security conscious; hence the keys on the body. He certainly went inside and changed because he was wearing the costume – which had been left out next to the freezer by Susanne – when he was found. According to the family, the light inside the barn had been switched off, but the door was still open because the body was blocking it.'

'He was obviously attacked before he could lock up.'

'Or, as Thulin suggested, he might have been hit just inside the barn and staggered out. But why didn't he have the sack of presents with him? They hadn't been touched.'

'If he was arguing with someone, maybe he was distracted,' Anita postulated. 'Stormed out of the barn, but intended going back in.'

'And the light?'

'If it was Sundin who turned off the light, that suggests he wasn't going to go back in, which contradicts what we just said about the presents. So, it's reasonable to speculate that the murderer switched it off. The light's not very strong, but it's enough to cast a faint beam in the direction of the body, and the killer couldn't close the door because it was in the way. Presumably, the perpetrator knew that Tord was expected to reappear in the house at four, so wanted as much time as possible to get away from the scene of the crime before his body was discovered. Which brings us to our suspects.'

'Well, on the family front, I'm pretty sure it's not Tord's wife who killed him,' Hakim began. 'She was seen most of the time and appeared, on the surface at least, distraught by her husband's death.'

'But you're not totally ruling her out?'

'No,' Hakim said guardedly. 'I admit she's got a motive. The family all seem to agree that Tord treated her badly. Her chance to break free?'

'There's another possible motive as well.'

'Really?' Hakim sounded surprised.

'Felicia Thorsson. But we'll come to her later.'

Hakim shrugged; he thought Anita was probably backing the wrong horse there, but no doubt she would come up with a good reason. 'As for the kids, none of the older ones are exactly heartbroken. Not a tear in sight. If one is to believe all that they told me tonight, then Tord Sundin comes across as a complete bastard. A bully who didn't care about his family. Everything had to revolve around him. Elvira talked about him playing "mind games" with people. He mucked up all their Christmas plans in one way or another. He had arguments with both Mårten and Susanne. Mårten dismissed it as nothing unusual. Susanne stormed out on her father according to Elvira, and when I asked her, she didn't attempt to deny it. But is their dislike enough to commit murder? Not really. That said; Mårten, Elvira and Susanne were all conveniently by themselves around the time the murder was committed. Mårten and Elvira were in their rooms, and Susanne had gone out for a walk to ring her boyfriend.'

Anita stretched out her legs. She was tired and wanted to head for bed, but they needed to round things up. 'So, all three have opportunity and vague motives.' She didn't bother to suppress a yawn. 'Actually, it's the Thorssons that interest me. Mismatched couple. Arne's a bit straight-laced, and yet he's ended up with a naturally flighty wife. I think he's uncomfortable with that, and he was upset by Tord's remark about her. That's why he went out of the house. Did he confront a drunken Tord in the yard? And then things got out of hand and he accidently killed him?'

'If so, he might have had the mysterious murder weapon on him. That would make it premeditated.'

Anita sat up. 'When we have an idea what we're looking for, we'll search both houses. As for Felicia...' She rubbed her eyes, trying to keep the tiredness at bay for a few more minutes. 'Felicia said she took Tord's comments in her stride. Was there something more to their relationship?'

'An affair?'

'That did occur to me. It would give Arne an added motive if Tord was flaunting the affair in front of him. That would also bring Barbara Sundin back into the picture. His comment about Felicia's breasts could have been the final mortification.'

'The girls certainly don't like Felicia. Susanne was very rude about her. Called her a "tart". If something was going on between them, could one of the kids have taken it upon themselves to put a stop to their mother's humiliation by doing something about it?' Anita could see the excitement in Hakim's eyes. Had she been like this on her early cases? She hoped that his enthusiasm would last as long as possible, before he was eventually worn down by policing that was over-bureaucratic and a legal system that seemed to go out of its way not to support the enforcers of the law.

'We mustn't dismiss Felicia either.'

'Why?'

'What if she and Tord had had an affair? As in past tense. Say he had dumped her. Felicia looks like a woman who likes to get her own way. Rejection is hard to take. Maybe his dodgy remark was a slap in the face? A woman scorned and all that.' Again, Hakim appeared dubious. He had already written Felicia off. 'Never discount anybody until you're a hundred per cent certain. Believe me; I've done it too often for comfort.'

Hakim blushed as he realized that Anita was getting to know him so well she could read his thoughts. 'OK, you're right. Felicia's still in. All are potential suspects. But what about Susanne's mysterious figure?'

'I was afraid you were going to mention that again,' Anita groaned. 'We'll have to look into the possibility that someone else was around. If that's the case, then maybe Arne saw something on *his* walk.' Anita clicked her fingers as a thought struck her. 'Both Arne and Susanne say they were wandering around at roughly the same time. Did they see each other? They could supply one another with alibis if they did,' she added reflectively. 'Or was it Arne that Susanne saw?'

'No.' Hakim wagged a finger at her. 'No. She said she saw the figure just before she heard the shouting. When she got to the barn, Mårten and Arne were already there. So it wasn't him.'

'Right. So we may have a possible stranger hanging around at the time.' Another yawn crept up on her, which she couldn't suppress. 'Sorry. God, I need my bed. You can have Lasse's old room.'

'Are you sure?'

Anita stood up and went over to the window. She peered through the blinds. Christmas Day morning. It was snowing again. 'You can't go out in this.'

'What should we do next? With the case.' Hakim was still in a state of exuberance.

'Well, I'll go down to headquarters tomorrow – or should I say "today"? – and do the relevant paperwork.'

'I'm covering again, so I'll have to be in, too.'

'That's fine. We can go down together. We'll have the place to ourselves.'

'But shouldn't we be going back and re-interviewing all our suspects?' She could see he was dying to get his teeth into the case.

'No. Let them stew for a while. They're not going to go anywhere as long as we have a police presence down there. Hopefully, that'll stop the killer, if it *is* one of them, getting rid of the murder weapon. We need to hear Eva Thulin's findings first. She might come up with some idea of what was used to kill him. What we also need to do is to find out more about them all. Some ammunition we can use. Have any of them got criminal records? Or have there been any previous altercations? I'll be interested in the backgrounds of the Thorssons. And if the killer is our stranger, then we need to dig deep into Tord Sundin's past.'

Anita had now got to the stage when she was almost too tired to sleep. She tossed and turned in her bed. She tried to think of positive things so her mind would just drift into a slumber. How were Lasse and Jazmin getting on in Tenerife? He had texted her that morning to say "Happy Christmas", but that was about it, other than to say it was warm. Maybe she should have gone with them. She could do with a dose of vitamin D. Not that Lasse would want his mamma around. She smiled to herself as she thought of Hakim sleeping in Lasse's room. It was nice to have a young person about the apartment, even if only for one night. And then her thoughts darkened as the realization came to her that she was leading a lonely life outside work. No one to share her thoughts with or go out and do things with – no one to hold her when she needed a hug, or to laugh with about the daft things in life. She suddenly missed Kevin. Though she had got used to not sharing her bed since her divorce, it had been good having Kevin by her side last summer. She would ring him in the morning, even though she knew that Christmas Day itself was a bigger deal in England than over here and that he would probably be heavily involved in whatever his family had got lined up for him. Then she smiled; knowing Kevin, he'd welcome the distraction. Well, this had certainly been one of her more eventful Christmas Eves; at least, the first with a murder attached. While the country was gathered round their festive tables after the visit by *tomten*, she had been intruding into the lives of a family whose Christmas had gone horribly wrong. Her mind was slipping back to the case. She grunted and turned over, pulling the duvet tightly up to her chin. Despite trying to force it from her mind, she couldn't help feeling that this investigation wasn't as straightforward as a simple family feud.

CHAPTER 10

Christmas Day was frustrating. In the strangely quiet polishus, Anita and Hakim trawled through the records; the only nugget they could find on the family was that Mårten had been involved in a fracas five years earlier when a group of lads had got into a scuffle outside a city bar. One arrest was made, but it wasn't Mårten. The reason for the skirmish might have been racist, as some of the names of the kids involved were Middle Eastern, but no one was too keen to highlight the fact. Maybe that's why there weren't more arrests. Whether that meant Mårten had a short fuse or was prone to violence couldn't be surmised from the report. And they couldn't find out more, as no one was around to ask. Finding nothing on Tord Sundin was more disappointing, as Anita thought that might provide them with a different angle. And to make it more exasperating, they knew that they wouldn't get anything from forensics for at least a couple of days. If Thulin could come up with a possible murder weapon, it might help. So, they ended up speculating yet again with much the same results. The two parking tickets that Felicia Thorsson had received in the last year didn't exactly point to a criminal past, but it did set them reassessing the neighbour:

'You still think Felicia Thorsson might be involved in this?' This was Hakim after they had started on their umpteenth coffee. The weak sunshine brightened the room but made little impact on the carpet of snow over Rörsjöparken and, according to the thermometer outside Anita's office window, the temperature was still below freezing.

'I suppose I do. The members of the family might have hated Tord, but I can't see a strong motive for actually killing him. It takes something else to commit patricide. Or mariticide for that matter.' She waved her hand at Hakim, who was looking sceptical again. 'I know, I know... but I'm not ruling Barbara out. That's why I'm more interested in the Thorssons. Love and sex can be a lethal mix.'

'A jealous Arne?'

'Exactly. We need to establish if the relationship between Tord and his bosomy buddy went beyond harmless flirtation. That would open up a few possibilities and certainly bring Arne to the front of the queue.' She stood up and stretched. She still felt tired after a restless night. 'By the way, did you find anything on Arne?'

'No criminal record. But he's a reasonably wealthy man. He still runs a small plastics firm in town. It was started by his father and he's run it since the late 1980s. He had to lay off some staff seven years ago, but they still seem to be making a profit, though I suspect that Felicia's doing her best to eat into that.' Anita laughed; she could see that. 'I've drawn a blank with Felicia so far. Don't know what her background is; whether she's been married before, what she did before she met Arne, or even where she's from. She doesn't have a Scanian accent. Need to get onto the tax people, but they won't be open until tomorrow at the earliest.'

Anita took her glasses off and made an industrious effort to clean them with the sleeve of her mauve jersey. When she was satisfied that she could see through them properly, she popped them back on. 'I can see you're straining at the leash. Go on; get yourself over to the Sundins'.' Hakim grinned. 'See if you can discover anything on the Tord-Felicia friendship. Best ask the kids; nothing in front of Barbara at this stage. And try to have a word with young Georg – did he see much of his mamma during the hour the Disney programme was on? Once Elvira had left the kitchen, Barbara may have been alone long enough to slip out and hit her husband. I know that "interviewing" Georg might be difficult, as you need to have an adult present; you could get that woman constable to sit in with you if she's around.'

Hakim drained his coffee and got ready to leave the office.

'One other thing. Two actually. Ask Susanne if she saw Arne when she was wandering around phoning her boyfriend. And while you're at it, get the boyfriend's full name. Tord may have been a pig, but he might well have had a good reason to disapprove of Susanne's young man.'

The drive to the Sundins' home in the pool car was easier than it had been the previous evening. Everywhere in the city, there was thick snow, but the roads had been cleared. At least he had a good idea of what he needed to establish, though he felt that Anita was letting herself be unnecessarily sidetracked by the Thorssons. The answer lay within the immediate family group; of that he was sure. And Mårten was *his* number one suspect. But disliking someone wasn't a sure-fire way of detecting a criminal. He had enough self-awareness to realize that he was being influenced by the fact that he knew one of the other names of those involved in the fight outside the pub. It was another Iraqi boy who had been the year behind him at his school in Rosengård. Whether the police were willing to admit it or not, Hakim was convinced that the incident had had racist overtones.

On his arrival, Hakim checked in with the constable who was on duty. There was nothing to report, and all the family were at home. He said that Mårten was doing something to his motorbike round the back.

The light was beginning to fade and Hakim could make out Tord's elder son, wearing a pair of overalls, bending over his bike. As he approached, Mårten glanced up, an oily cloth in his hand.

'Are you going to keep us bottled up here forever?' the young man said testily. 'I'm back at work the day after tomorrow.'

'I'm sure that won't be a problem. As long as we know where you are.'

'Why? Do you think I'll run away?' he said acerbically as he turned his attention back to the bike.

'Do you have a reason to?'

'No,' he snapped back. There was a flash of temper. The mucky cloth was crumpled into a ball in his strong fingers. This was an irascible young man. Had his father sparked the same anger the day before?

'You seem to have been involved in a violent incident a few years back.'

Mårten stopped what he was doing and slowly rose to his feet. He turned to face Hakim – he was as tall as the police officer but had broader shoulders; he was an intimidating sight. 'It was nothing. I wasn't even arrested. Look, say what you want to say and then leave me alone.' He stared resentfully at Hakim – an immigrant and a policeman: two particulars obviously invidious to the hostile Mårten.

Hakim turned up the collar of his coat. It was cold and he'd rather do this indoors, but it was an opportunity to question Mårten out of his mother's hearing. And at least today he was wearing a pair of fleece-lined boots. They had belonged to Lasse, and Anita had dug them out for him that morning to replace the still-sodden suede shoes. Hakim's inclination was to press the boy further about his argument with his father yesterday morning. However, he didn't want to report back to Anita that he hadn't found out the information she had sent him to get.

'Your father. Was he having a relationship with Felicia Thorsson?'

'It wouldn't surprise me. But I don't know. In the last few

years, I haven't been around here much, especially when he was at home. Often stayed over with mates in town.' Then he laughed. 'Do you think she battered him to death with those knockers of hers?'

Hakim ignored the remark. 'We're trying to build up a picture of your father, that's all. We need to find the reason why he was killed.'

Suddenly, Mårten's tone was serious. 'If you think it's Mamma, forget it. Even if he was playing around – and I'm sure he shagged his way through the brothels of Hong Kong or Chennai or wherever his ships docked – Mamma would have turned a blind eye. That's just her way of coping. Always has been. Despite everything, she loved him.' He went silent for a moment. All Hakim could hear was Mårten's slow breathing. 'Maybe one day she'll realize that she's better off without him, but I doubt it.'

Was this the beginnings of a confession? Hakim wondered. 'Did you kill him to protect your mother?' The light had faded so quickly, they were now almost in the dark, and he couldn't see the boy's reaction.

'I don't kill people, however obnoxious.'

Elvira Sundin wasn't as belligerent as her brother. Of the three older offspring of Tord Sundin, she appeared to be the most affected by his death. Whether that was simply because of the sheer horror of the situation, or whether it was out of concern for her mother, Hakim wasn't sure; probably a bit of both. But she seemed more willing to discuss the events than the others.

'I'm not sure,' she said in answer to his question as to whether her father had had an affair with Felicia Thorsson. 'He made no secret of fancying her, but men do that without thinking,' she said with a slight edge of disgust. 'I haven't been around that much in recent years. Happy to stay up in Gothenburg; even during the holidays.'

'But, he could have had an affair?' Hakim pressed.

They had the kitchen to themselves. The television was playing loudly next door. Barbara was indulging Georg with one of his favourite films; fortunately, it ensured that she couldn't hear what they were saying.

'I suppose. I hope not. It would have killed Mamma. She's taken this whole thing very badly. Heard her crying all last night. I suppose she still loved him.'

'Mårten thought that even if she had known, she would have turned a blind eye.'

Elvira looked incredulous. 'I doubt it. Mamma has her pride. OK, Dad trampled over it a lot, but when pushed to the limit, she has a temper.' Realizing that Hakim might take this the wrong way, she hurried on, 'Not in a violent way at all. Just that she could get cross on occasions.'

'You reckon she would have confronted him if she'd known about an affair?'

'Possibly,' she said quietly. 'But we don't know that he was having one.'

'I understand what you're saying, but it could have happened? Your mother works part-time, doesn't she?'

'Yes. She was a nurse when she met Dad. Still works two days a week at a surgery off Ystadvägen.'

'So, she must have gone to work when your dad was home from sea. And, as I assume Felicia doesn't work...' – this was confirmed by Elvira's raised eyebrows and a slight inclination of her head – 'and Arne does, there would have been easy opportunities for them to get together.'

Elvira shrugged helplessly. Hakim saw that there was no further point speculating. If she knew anything, she wasn't telling.

'OK, thank you. I'll have a word with your sister.'

Elvira visibly relaxed. 'She's in her room.'

'That smells nice,' Hakim said as he made to leave the

kitchen. Whatever was cooking, it was making him hungry.

'It's fish soup. None of us have much of an appetite, so I got something easy from the freezer.'

'*Bon appetit!* Oh, just one more thing: you haven't been aware of anything odd happening around here since you came back?'

'Like what?'

'It's just that your sister said that she thought she saw someone outside not long after we think the murder took place.'

Elvira screwed up her face. 'No. Nothing.' She paused and looked contemplative. 'Well... perhaps there was one thing. The night before Dad came back – my first night here – I was woken by the noise of a car about two in the morning. But it was probably the Thorssons coming back late from a Christmas party or something.'

Hakim had to knock on Susanne's bedroom door several times before it was opened. The reason was immediate. She had earphones clamped to each side of her head, and still the music was thudding away. This time there was no smile or "cute" remark. He could see that his interruption was resented.

'This won't take long.' This did nothing to placate Susanne, who slumped on her bed. 'Turn that off, please,' he had to add loudly.

She made great play of stopping the music and she took one earphone out. The other stayed obstinately in place. She had made no effort to dress smartly today, and she looked more comfortable in the skinny ripped jeans and sloppy blue singlet. The Christmas jumper had been unceremoniously discarded, lying crumpled on the floor in front of the wardrobe. Hakim suspected it would never be worn again. Susanne was glowering.

'When you went out for your wander to phone your boyfriend, did you see Arne Thorsson?'

'No,' she mumbled.

'Are you sure?'

'Yes,' she snarled back.

Hakim wondered if Arne had seen her, or were they both lying? 'By the way, can I have your boyfriend's second name? Lucas what?'

'Why?' she demanded. 'He has nothing to do with this.'

'Name, please,' Hakim persisted stubbornly.

When she eventually spoke: 'Drakenberg.'

'Where does he live?'

'Why are you asking this?'

'We have to check out everyone's story.' Hakim's biro was poised over his notepad.

'Söderkulla. He lives in Östra Söderkulla.' It was like pulling teeth. Hakim was beginning to wonder if it was even worth asking her about Felicia Thorsson.

'Right, just one last thing.' Susanne sighed heavily as though she were being asked to do some arduous chore. 'Do you know if your father was having an affair with Felicia next door?'

To his surprise, she brightened up. 'Yeah! Of course he was screwing her! Why do you think we hate her so much?'

'How do you know they were... you know?'

'At it?' she scoffed. 'Can't you say it?' she mocked. 'I saw them once. Well, heard, actually. Mamma was at work and I came back early from school. I could hear them up in Mamma's bedroom. Well, the bitch. She was yelping and screaming at the top of her voice and then I heard my dad pleading for her to keep the noise down. It would have been funny if it hadn't been so tragic. How could he do it in the bed that Mamma sleeps in? It was nauseating. Filthy bastard!' There was real fury in her voice.

'You're sure it was Felicia?'

'Oh, yes. I saw her leave out the back shortly afterwards. And the next time he was home from sea, I saw him sneaking out of her place in the middle of the afternoon looking like a cat that had got the cream. Arne wasn't around.'

'Did anybody else know?'

'Elvira.'

'Elvira?' Hakim remarked in surprise. She'd been reticent on the subject.

'Saw them banging away in the wood behind the house once.'

'And was it still going on? The affair?'

'What?' Her anger had temporarily taken her to another place. 'The affair?' She thought for a moment. 'Now you mention it, he was a bit off with her yesterday. He was still slobbering, as he always did. But now I come to think about it, there was something not quite right.' Then a gleam came into her pale blue eyes. 'You don't think the bitch killed him?'

'We're looking into every possibility,' said Hakim as he closed his notebook and slipped it into his coat pocket. 'Ah, there was something else – have you had any more thoughts on the figure you might or might not have seen?'

Susanne was almost convivial now. 'I have actually. I definitely think someone was around. But who it could have been, I have no idea.' She whipped out the other earphone and stared hard at Hakim, eyes wide. 'It could have been *her*.'

'You didn't hear anything on the night before your father came back? A car? About two in the morning?'

'No,' she said emphatically. 'Dead to the world. Who said something about a car?'

'Elvira.'

'Wouldn't listen to her. Probably been smoking too much weird stuff. You know what these students are like.'

As Hakim thoughtfully made his way back to Anita's Peugeot, a squad car pulled up. He recognized the constable getting out – it was Liv Fogelström. As she walked forward in the glare of the headlights, she gave him a big smile, which he found gave him a slight buzz.

'I've come to relieve my colleague. I'm on night duty.'

'Sorry about that, but Inspector Sundström thinks it's a necessary precaution.' He gazed at her as though seeing her for the first time. She had a pleasing, slightly chubby face. Rounded cheek bones above a wide mouth helped to accentuate an infectious grin. Her blonde hair was scraped back into a plait under her regulation "boat" cap. 'I'm sure it won't last long.' He knew it couldn't. Once Christmas was over, some senior officer would notice the expensive overtime and come knocking on Anita's door demanding to know why.

'Good. It's a bit boring.'

Hakim found himself apologizing again and, for some reason that he couldn't explain, he wanted to continue talking to Liv Fogelström. He didn't know what to say, but he made no move to go.

'I'd better get on,' Fogelström said, breaking the silence. 'David won't want to hang around here any longer. He's a family to go back to.'

'Of course.' He watched her trudge in her heavy boots up the snowy rutted road towards the Sundin property. Then he remembered something: he hadn't spoken to Georg. That would have to wait.

The drive back into Malmö was disconcerting. While he was trying to think about the case and how the interviews had panned out, the face of the young constable kept intruding. Not that that in itself was unpleasant or even annoying – just distracting. But by the time he was close to the polishus, his mind was refocused on the murder. And what was now whirling around in his head was a fresh theory. On the face of it, an unlikely scenario, but it also made sense, and fitted the facts as he knew them. Whether Anita would buy it was another matter.

CHAPTER 11

Anita had waited at the polishus for Hakim's return. She had to admit she'd spent more enjoyable Christmas Days. As expected, she hadn't got much further with unearthing any more relevant information about their suspects, as all the people she needed to speak to were on holiday. The festive season was a good time to murder someone. While Hakim was out, she'd taken the opportunity to ring Kevin to wish him a happy Christmas. He was obviously pleased she'd called. He wanted to know when she was coming over to Penrith to visit him. She vaguely promised that she might try and get across in March – she had some leave coming up then. As she rang off, she could tell that he was about to say something more personal, but he stopped himself – perhaps he was within earshot of one of his daughters or his ex-wife. But she finished the conversation with a smile on her face.

Anita was further enthused by Hakim's confirmation of the affair between Tord Sundin and Felicia Thorsson. Mårten thought it was possible, but it was Susanne who had caught them at it – or heard them at it to be precise. And Elvira had actually seen them, according to her sister, yet hadn't admitted it to Hakim. Was she trying to hide something? Anita drained her last coffee of the day and lobbed the paper cup into the bin. 'I thought so! It really does put a different spin on the situation.'

'I know that puts Arne in the frame,' Hakim agreed, 'but your hunch about Felicia might also be right. Susanne thought there was something odd going on between her dad and Felicia when the Thorssons came across for their drinks. A falling-out between lovers, possibly?'

'Interesting. Anyway, that gives us something to go on.' As she stood up, she blew out her cheeks. Time to go home. 'Only problem is, it gives us yet more suspects.' She took her coat off the back of her chair and wriggled into it. 'Do you want to come back to mine tonight?'

'No thanks. Better pop round to my parents'. See how they're surviving.'

'OK. I'll give you a lift.'

They made their way down Nobelvägen. The street was coming to life after a quiet day. The snow had turned slushy and was now starting to freeze. Anita just wanted to get home and relax in front of the telly with a glass of wine and the big box of chocolates that Lasse had left her. She turned onto Ystadvägen briefly before she pulled into Sofielund, where the familiar, red-brick apartment block that Hakim had lived in with his parents when she had first got to know him was located. She noted that the area had been spruced up since she had last been there; it was now more pedestrian-friendly with wider pavements, and areas set aside for grass or seasonal planting. It might even look half-decent in the summer. Anita drew up in front of the glass front door.

'Do you want to come in?' Hakim asked.

Anita knew she should if only because of Lasse and Jazmin, but she couldn't face the thought of socializing. 'I'll pass, if you don't mind. But give them my best wishes.'

Hakim moved to get out of the car, but a visible reluctance kept him in his seat.

'Something on your mind?'

Hakim gave her a rueful smile. 'Well, yes. This may sound ridiculous, but when I was talking to the Sundin children, they all came out with the same thing in one way or another – their protectiveness towards their mother. I mentioned this before; the feeling was even stronger this time.'

'Strong enough to do something about it?'

'Exactly! I know this is crazy, but could all three of them have been involved? I mean, working together. I don't know which one might have done the actual killing,' he hurried on before Anita shot his idea down, 'but they could have conspired together, determined to do something to end their mamma's humiliation once and for all.' Hakim turned to Anita expectantly. He was ready for the put-down.

'It's not such a stupid idea. But, if they did it together, don't you think they'd have given each other alibis?'

'I've thought about that. I think it was probably a last-minute decision. Remember, they didn't know he was coming back. And when he did, maybe it was his boorish behaviour that pushed them over the edge. When they'd done it, they didn't have much time to work out their alibis; well, only enough to put them all somewhere else at the time of the murder. It might explain why Tord didn't see the attack coming – one or two of them are talking to him and the third comes up behind and... whack! Maybe Susanne got rid of the murder weapon, which would explain why she was out in the wood.'

In the darkness, Hakim couldn't read Anita's expression.

'OK. Tomorrow you can check Susanne's phone records. Was she phoning her boyfriend as she said? And check him out, too.'

Hakim's mind was racing now. 'What... what if Barbara Sundin was in on it, too? The whole family? Except Georg, of course. It's feasible, isn't it?'

'Possibly,' Anita said softly. 'Put it this way, we can't discount anything at this stage.' She gave him a motherly pat on the knee.

'But now, go and see your parents.'

Liv Fogelström sat in the kitchen by herself. Fru Sundin had made her a thermos of coffee, which she had to admit was not only lovely and strong, but was also helping to keep her awake. Mårten and Elvira had been the last to go to bed. They had finished watching the TV at around midnight. Fogelström had gone outside and wandered round the house with a torch. She had also gone over to the Thorssons': no lights had been visible.

Despite the regular fixes of coffee, she found herself yawning. It was assignments like this that were so dull. She got out her smartphone and scrolled through it without really taking in what she was looking at, or even looking for. It was more of a reflex action. After tonight she was due three days off because she had worked over Christmas. First, a good sleep, then she would go over and visit her brother in Helsingborg and deliver her nephews' presents: a belated Christmas celebration. She idly wondered what someone like Inspector Mirza did at this time of year. Nothing, she supposed. Different religion. He had nice eyes. A kindly face. She wasn't so sure about the senior detective, Inspector Sundström. She'd heard some strange things about her; all sorts of scrapes and misdemeanours. She had the impression that she wasn't universally liked, but you could never tell with police station tittle-tattle.

She put her phone down and stretched. The digital cooker clock showed 02.14. She was to be relieved at six. Still nearly four hours. She leant over the table and took one of the home-made biscuits fru Sundin had left on a plate. As she took a bite, she tensed. Was that the sound of an engine? There was no through road beyond the houses, so any vehicle in the vicinity must be coming to either the Sundins' or the Thorssons'. She got to her feet and peered out of the kitchen window. She couldn't see anything. The torch was by the back door. She picked it up, flicked it on and ventured out. It was a cold, moonless night, and the cloud cover ensured that everything beyond the house was obfuscated. Only the light behind her from the kitchen and the thin beam of the torch in front of her illuminated the scene. She crunched her way tentatively through the snow round to the front of the house and shone her light down the track. Nothing. Turning round, she decided to make another recce of the properties. Both were in darkness. The first flakes of a fresh fall of snow began to spot her face. Coming round from the side of the Thorsson house, she started at the sound of a hooting owl. She smiled at her own jumpiness. Soon, she found herself at the back of the Sundins' barn. Her torch picked out the rear entrance. Unlike the one at the front of the building, this one, in order to make access easier, had a smaller aperture within one of the large, heavy main doors. Fogelström looked more closely. Was this smaller door slightly open? Had it been left like that? She was sure it had been closed when she had done her earlier rounds. She stood, rooted to the spot, and listened. All was still. There was no wind, and the oppressive, Cimmerian darkness enveloped her like a shroud. She chided herself for her own timidity. But she would have been more at ease if a colleague had been with her. Just in case. She stirred herself and cautiously approached the gap.

As she leant forward to push the door shut, she thought she heard a movement inside. Was it a trick of the night? These old buildings had voices all of their own. She held her breath. Instead of shutting the door, she slowly pulled it further open. It creaked loudly on its rusty hinges.

'Hello?' she called out, trying to suppress the tremor in her voice. 'Anybody there?' There wasn't a sound. She gingerly moved forward and stepped over the threshold. Then she felt a searing pain and her world went black.

CHAPTER 12

The first Anita knew about what had happened to Constable Fogelström was when she arrived in her office the morning after Christmas Day. She had given herself a short lie-in, which she immediately felt guilty about when she saw a shaken Hakim.

'Liv Fogelström was attacked in the night! She's in hospital.'

'Who's Liv Fogelström?'

'The constable who was on duty last night down at the Sundins' house.'

Now she realized the gravity of the news. 'Right, let's get down there now.'

On the way, Hakim brought her up to speed. The replacement constable had arrived at six o'clock as scheduled and couldn't find any trace of Fogelström. He had woken the family, and they had searched for her. Mårten had found her bound and gagged at the back of the barn behind where the Volvo was parked. Like Tord, she had been hit over the head. But, unlike Tord, she was still alive and semi-conscious, though understandably badly shaken by the incident, and an ambulance had been called to take her to Malmö's Skåne University Hospital. Apparently, none of the family had heard anything during the night. The first they were aware of something being wrong was when they were woken by the policeman.

On their arrival, Anita and Hakim could see two police

cars, and a number of officers milling around. It was Constable Reuben Persson, whom they had met on the first night of the case, who greeted them.

'How is Liv? Er... Fogelström,' Hakim quickly corrected himself. Anita gave him a sidelong look.

'The medics say she'll be OK; it's not life-threatening.'

'Let's go to the barn,' Anita prompted.

They followed Persson. They worked their way between the car and the large freezer to the back door.

'This is where she was found. Tied up in that corner,' Persson explained.

Anita glanced round the barn. 'And where does this door lead to?' As she spoke, she tried the latch. It was locked.

'Outside. The back.'

'Do we know what she was doing in here? Or was she attacked somewhere else and dragged in?'

'Not sure. She was too shaken to speak... the blow and everything.' Anita couldn't help but notice Hakim blanch.

'And you've spoken to the family?'

'Between us we have. No one heard anything.'

Anita could see that Hakim had been upset by the whole incident. Best to get him out of the way. 'Hakim, can you go and have another word with the Sundins and the Thorssons? Someone must have heard something. Fogelström must have been out here for a reason.'

'She might have just been doing her rounds,' suggested Persson. 'That's what we've been doing each night.'

'I know. But she obviously disturbed someone.' Hakim left the barn.

'So, who did she disturb?' Anita ruminated again. 'What was going on in here last night?' She went over to the side door that she'd noticed on her original visit. Tord Sundin had had the barn keys on him when he died. She turned to Persson: 'I want to have a look in there. Where are the keys?'

69

'Inspector Mirza has them.'

'Just go and get them off him, would you?'

As she glanced round the barn, she couldn't help thinking about this strange development. Could it be their killer who had attacked Fogelström? Same MO. But if one of the family had wanted to escape for a while, why go to this extreme? And if had they wanted to get away, what for? To get rid of the murder weapon? That was a thought. She found herself opening the freezer again. It was two-thirds full of provisions: meat, fish and some boxes of unidentifiable foodstuffs, possibly vegetables or fruit preserved from the summer. It reminded Anita that she was going to have to stock up her own food supplies, which were virtually non-existent. Persson interrupted her when he came back brandishing a set of keys. All of them were for mortise locks. He tried one; it didn't fit. The second time, he was luckier.

Now Anita could see that the barn was indeed huge; the garage area was just a fraction of its full size. Standing outside, it had been difficult to appreciate how vast it was. The section on the other side of the internal door was used for storage. It had two small windows on opposite walls, which were grimy and covered in cobwebs, letting in little light. Suspended from the roof was another, rather pathetic, lone light bulb, which wasn't even centrally situated; it hung limply not far from the door. As Hakim had previously reported, the place was full of the kind of bric-a-brac that people accumulate and then store because they don't know what to do with it or are reluctant to dispose of it. This was the preserve of the old and dusty, the neglected, broken and unwanted. There were bits of furniture – a wardrobe, an old-fashioned dressing table, chairs of various sorts and a large sofa that had half the seat stuffing missing. A stack of boxes was piled in one corner; old sports equipment and fishing rods lay about in a dispirited kind of way – there was even an abandoned car engine. The only things that looked used were some gardening tools and the mower that Hakim had spotted. On a genuinely distressed table, there were some old LPs and a couple of mouldy boxes containing board games. Anita recognized Cluedo – she'd always hated it! Then something under the table caught her eye. Unlike everything else, this looked clean. She picked it up. It was a nice little thing – a small ivory figure of an old man bending down, cradling a child. It had two small, adjacent, interconnecting holes in the back of it. Was it Chinese? Japanese? She wasn't sure. Probably it was something Tord had brought back from one of his voyages. She put the figure on the table and scanned the area again. Nothing that was an obvious murder weapon. Then again, as Hakim had said, the murder weapon couldn't have been in here: Tord Sundin had had the key on him and the door had been locked. She mooched around a bit more. She knew Tord had come to the barn to change into his costume and pick up the presents, but they'd been put in the garage by Susanne, and he'd had no reason to come in here. She sat on one of the chairs and stared into the gloom. At that moment, the sun came out and a single dust-bespattered beam shot through the front window. That was it! That's what was missing! Now she began to search more frantically. Eventually, in one of the boxes, she found what she had been looking for. Santa's beard.

'OK,' Anita said decisively. 'Lock this room up and let's have a look outside the back door.'

The tract of ground between the barn and the road must have been about seventy metres long. It was covered in last night's snow, and a pale sun gleamed off the crinkled surface, which reminded Anita of the icing on a Christmas cake one of their neighbours in Britain had once given them.

'There's been a vehicle here,' observed Persson.

'Yes. But how long ago? Difficult to tell.'

The snow had obscured the pattern left by the tread of the tyres, but the indentations were clear.

'Wide tyres – large car, SUV; or could be a van,' said Persson.

'Collecting something?' Anita mused. 'And no one heard anything?'

Persson shrugged. 'That's what they say.'

'It doesn't appear to have turned. Backed up from the road?' Who was up here and why? Anita pondered as she examined the ground. She went back through the door and bent down on her haunches to have a closer look at the tyres of the Volvo. Definitely not wide enough. And the earth floor looked dry.

'It wasn't this one, anyhow. Right. Get onto forensics. I need them down here to check this ground out. Not easy with the snow, I grant you, but we might be lucky.'

Persson left the barn to phone as Hakim came the other way. He was shaking his head. 'Nothing. All the bedrooms, except Susanne's, are at the other end of the house. And Susanne says she goes to sleep with her music on, so never hears anything.'

'Well, I think I've got something. I knew Sundin didn't look quite right.'

Hakim squinted quizzically at her, a hand coming up to shade his eyes from the sun.

'OK, there was a lump on his head and he was lying on the ground. But there was something else: where was his beard? *Tomten* always wears a beard. Sundin's was in a box in the storage area.'

'So he could have gone in there after all!' Hakim looked impressed.

'All right,' Anita got back down to business. 'A vehicle was parked round the back, through there.' She indicated the door that was ajar at the back of the barn. 'Can't tell if it was there last night. It's not their Volvo, so someone came visiting.'

'You know, Elvira didn't hear anything this time, but she said she heard a vehicle of some sort in the early hours of the night before her father arrived back. About two, she said. She thought it might have been the Thorssons coming back from a pre-Christmas party.'

Anita grinned back at him. 'Well, that's another thing I can ask Felicia. About time I had another personal chitchat. She's got a lot to get off her chest.'

Felicia was wearing white slacks and a figure-hugging, sky-blue sweater. Both were too tight, and the bulges at her waistline showed that maybe a post-Christmas diet might be in order. Anita herself had been recently buying clothes a size up from her normal ten; it was easier than losing weight. Felicia wasn't pleased to see her and reluctantly let her in. Arne sat quietly in the corner of the living room gazing out of the window. There was an uncomfortable ambience in the room, which indicated that a row had taken place. Anita had had enough of them with her ex-husband, Björn, to pick up the vibes.

'I'd like to speak to your wife alone, herr Thorsson.'

Arne gazed at her for a moment, then got up and left without a word.

'He can be a miserable sod sometimes,' said Felicia, flinging herself onto the sofa with an exaggerated sigh. Then she sat up.

'Park your bum.' Anita sat down in a chair opposite. Before she had time to ask her first question, Felicia pre-empted her: 'You're here about me and Tord, aren't you? Don't look surprised. When someone says "I'd like to speak to your wife alone", it's fairly obvious. So, who told you?'

'One of the family heard you. You were very loud.'

Felicia giggled. 'Men like that sort of thing. The louder you yell, the more satisfaction they think they're giving you. I'm sure you know. Bollocks, of course. Anyway, I bet it was Elvira. Little snake. All nice as pie on the surface, but a stuck-up cow. Just because she's at university, she thinks she's better than people like me.'

'Doesn't matter who it was. The point is that you lied to me about your relationship.'

'A girl has to have her secrets.'

'How long had it been going on?'

Felicia stood up and moved over to a table upon which was a pearl- inlaid wooden box. She took out a cigarette and lit it with a silver lighter. She took a huge puff before returning to her seat. 'He hates this,' she said, breathing out a plume of smoke. Anita wished that Felicia hadn't lit up, as it awakened suppressed urges. She hadn't had a cigarette for over two years; or snus since the start of the summer.

'A few years.'

'A few years?' Anita repeated in surprise. 'But you haven't been married to Arne that long.'

'I met Tord before I met Arne. On holiday.' She took another deep drag on her cigarette. 'In Thailand. His ship had come into Singapore. He didn't have time to get back to Europe before his next ship out, so he popped up to Ao Nang for a few days' rest and recreation. I was the recreation. There were other Swedes there and we got on. A holiday fling. Nothing else.' She leant over and stubbed out the half-smoked cigarette in an expensive porcelain ashtray. Anita was relieved that she had finished. 'Then I met Arne out there, too. It came up in conversation that he was Tord's neighbour. I was looking to settle down. A girl can't keep the wolf from the door for ever, and even one's obvious charms begin to fade, so I didn't want to hang around.'

'So, you snared poor old Arne?'

'"Snared" is a very judgmental word. Coaxed. Not that he needed much coaxing. He's done well out of it. He's never had better sex, and I show him how to spend his money.'

'And you had the extra benefit of having Tord as an occasional distraction.'

She cackled this time. 'You should have seen Tord's face when I rolled up. Gobsmacked, I think you'd call it. We just carried on as before, but we did try and keep it discreet. I didn't want to upset Arne.'

'And kill the golden goose.'

'That's a bit harsh. Besides, I like Barbara. She's been kind to me.'

Despite all the awful things she was saying, Anita found herself warming to Felicia's honest brashness. 'And had it finished?'

Felicia gave Anita a sharp look. 'What makes you think that?'

'Just the impression I get.' Anita knew she was fishing, but Felicia seemed to be in confessional mode.

'Ever had an affair with a married man?'

The question caught Anita off her guard. It was a few moments before she replied: 'No.'

'You've missed out. I recommend it. The errant husband is so desperate for it, that he treats you like a queen. And there are no complications because he'll go to a helluva lot of trouble not to be discovered by his wife, which leaves you in the clear.'

'And what makes you think Barbara didn't know?'

It was Felicia's turn to look appalled. 'Did she?'

Anita wasn't going to tell her one way or the other. 'Tord didn't seem the sort of person who would be too fussed if his wife knew. From what we've gathered, he didn't treat Barbara with much respect.'

Felicia arched an eyebrow. 'He could be a bit of a tyrant, but he didn't want her to know he was being a naughty boy. They'd been through a lot together.'

Anita sat forward in her seat. 'You still haven't answered my question.'

'Persistent, aren't you? Yes, it had finished. Well, that was the impression I had when we went over there on Christmas Eve. He didn't say anything about it directly, but I've been given the brush-off enough to read the runes.'

'And were you upset?'

Her smile was filled with melancholy. 'I suppose I was. I was up for a bit of slap and tickle. Arne's a lovely man, but he's no great shakes between the sheets. A girl needs a good gallop from time to time. I have to say, in my defence, that Tord is the only man I've been unfaithful with since marrying Arne. And that doesn't really count because we were lovers before I met my husband.' For sheer brass neck, Felicia was in a class of her own.

'Did you kill Tord?'

Felicia's eyes narrowed as she surveyed the police inspector sitting alertly opposite her. 'You don't beat about the bush, do you? You probably have to be like that to survive in the police. Bet it's a hard environment for a woman. Well, you've been direct with me, so I'll be direct with you. I didn't kill Tord.'

Anita got to her feet. 'What about your husband?'

'You can't ask a wife that.'

'I just have.'

Felicia eased back into the cushions. The rueful beam appeared again. 'Not Arne.'

'What makes you think he didn't do it out of jealousy?'

She shook her head vigorously. 'You've got it wrong. I admit he didn't like the way I flirted with Tord, and vice versa. But he didn't know we were having it off. Well, not until last night.'

'What happened last night?'

She raised her eyebrows and looked at a drinks tray on a small table. On it were a couple of bottles; one of gin and the other of whisky. There was only a smidgen of clear liquid at the bottom of the gin bottle. 'Too much of that. Got a bit maudlin. I was missing Tord. It just slipped out.'

'Hence the stony silence when I came in?'

'He'll get over it.'

Anita moved towards the door. 'Oh, by the way, were you out late the night before Tord got back? That would be the twenty-second. Returning round about two? A party or something?'

'Fat chance of that. No, I was well tucked up in my bed that night – like every other bloody night!'

CHAPTER 13

Anita left the Thorssons' house after having a brief word with a crestfallen Arne. She believed Felicia when she'd said that her husband had only found out about the affair last night, and Arne confirmed it. And even if Arne had suspected his wife of being unfaithful, he obviously hadn't had any evidence. Hardly a reason to kill someone, purely on conjecture. But Anita's feelings about Felicia were different. For all her apparent honesty, she wasn't sure she'd had the entire truth.

Anita had also asked Arne if he'd seen Susanne while out on his walk. He hadn't. So, neither could corroborate the other's story.

In the courtyard, she was met by Constable Persson. He seemed nervous.

'Sorry, Inspector, but no luck with forensics. They won't be able to get down today. Not enough people in. Holidays. There's been a shooting in Kroksbäck. They said dead bodies have priority. Tyre tracks come way down the list.'

'Damn.' Persson looked sheepish. 'Not your fault. OK, tape off that whole area. I don't want it disturbed until someone can be bothered to come down here.' This was really frustrating. The attack on Fogelström was a potential lead. But to what? Did it have anything to do with Tord Sundin's murder?

Persson hurried off just as Hakim appeared from the kitchen.

'Please give me some positive news,' Anita said, more in hope than expectation.

'A couple of things of interest,' countered Hakim. They began to walk towards the end of the house. 'Elvira confirmed Susanne had put both the Santa suit and the sack of presents beside the freezer the night before. They wanted them out of Georg's sight so he wouldn't discover them. The suit usually lives in the box where you found the beard. They wanted Tord to be able to lay his hands on everything easily. Susanne must just have missed the beard. The light's not brilliant in there at night.'

They rounded the corner of the building and made their way towards Anita's car. 'OK, so he might have gone into the storeroom to find the beard–'

'He spoke to someone outside on his way over there.'

Anita stopped abruptly: 'Who?'

'Felicia Thorsson.'

'You're joking!'

Hakim looked rather pleased with himself. 'I had a quiet word with Georg. He's a nice, young lad.'

'Was an adult present?'

He pretended to be horrified. 'Inspector Sundström, I wouldn't dream of interviewing someone under age without going through the proper procedure. I just came across him and we had a little, friendly natter. I wanted to see if he was OK.'

'You're learning fast, Inspector Mirza.'

'The poor kid is totally confused by his father's death. Actually, I don't think he really understands what has taken place. Anyway, he happened to mention that his mother and Elvira came in and out of the kitchen while he was watching his *Donald Duck* programme. Felicia was with him a lot of the time, but only after she returned from following his dad when he left to "go to the shops". That's the excuse Tord always used when he went out to dress up as Santa. Georg's just eight; he doesn't believe in *tomten* any more, but he goes along with it.

Anyway, he heard them talking quite loudly outside the living room window.'

'Did he hear what they said?'

Hakim shook his head. 'No. He just heard their voices. He said it was annoying, as he was trying to concentrate on the telly.'

Anita made for the car and pulled out her key. 'I knew she was holding something back.' She unlocked the door and opened it.

Hakim stood at the passenger side. 'Aren't you going to have another word with her now you know?'

'She can keep. I want to chivvy Eva Thulin along. We're stuck without a murder weapon. And I want a more precise time of death if possible.'

'What can I do?'

'I'm going to drop you off at the hospital. I want you to see if Fogelström is up to talking.' Hakim's eyes flitted away from Anita's gaze. 'I want to know if she can remember anything about last night.'

The hospital had made an effort to brighten things up with Christmas decorations and an enormous tree, almost reaching the foyer ceiling. Not that there was much festive spirit in the small side room that Liv Fogelström occupied. Hakim gulped when he saw the bandage that was wrapped round her head – and her wrists were covered, too, where she had been tied. She had her eyes shut, and he wasn't sure if she was asleep. As he stood awkwardly clutching a bunch of pink carnations, her eyes opened. Her face creased into a smile. Hakim wasn't sure what to do with the flowers – he had never bought any before, but he knew that was what was expected. Fortunately, a middle-aged nurse came in at that moment, saw the embarrassed young man's dilemma and took them from him. 'I'll put them in water.'

'How are you?' he asked, finding it difficult to look at

Fogelström directly.

'My head hurts,' she said, grimacing with the effort of speaking.

'I'm so sorry.' It was an inadequate response, but he didn't really know what to say to her. How could someone do such a thing to so lovely a girl? He would make sure he nailed the bastard.

'My fault.' She weakly raised her hand and pointed to a chair. Hakim pulled it across and sat next to the bed. He had never felt like this before, sitting so close to a woman about whom he couldn't rationalize his thoughts. He just knew that he wanted to be near her; to protect her. But he must get on with the business of his visit.

'Are you up to talking? About last night?'

Fogelström blinked and inclined her head almost imperceptibly. Just then the nurse came back in with the flowers in a cream and purple vase, which somewhat clashed with the colour of the petals. She put them carefully on the cabinet next to Fogelström's bed.

'Thank you,' said Hakim.

'I know you're here to ask questions, but go easy,' the nurse said severely. 'This young lady has had an awful experience and she needs rest. You've got five minutes, then I'll chase you out.'

'Yes, of course.' He waited for the nurse to leave before he spoke again. 'Fogelström... can you... Sorry, this sounds too formal in the circumstances.'

'It's Liv, Inspector.'

'I know.' She seemed pleased. Hakim waved his hand. 'And forget the "inspector" bit. I'm Hakim. In here, anyway,' he grinned conspiratorially. He coughed to clear his throat before proceeding. 'Last night? Do you remember anything?'

'Not much.' As she paused, he could see by the concentration on her face that she was desperately searching her memory for anything that could help.

'Why did you go out of the house when you did?' said Hakim in an attempt to prompt her thoughts.

After a few moments of reflection, she said: 'The engine.'

'What engine?'

'I heard the sound of an engine. I went to check.'

'Was the sound coming from near the barn?'

'I suppose so.'

'Which way did you go into the barn? Through the main doors?'

Fogelström frowned. 'No. No, I went round the back. The back of the barn.'

'That could be right. There's a door there. Inspector Sundström reckons there was a vehicle there last night.'

'There was something wrong. But I can't remember what it was.'

Hakim didn't like pushing her, but he knew he had to. 'Was there something wrong outside? Or something wrong with the door?'

Then recognition gradually eased across her face. 'It was the door. It was ajar. That's right. I must have stepped in to have a look.' She looked at him appealingly. 'I'm so sorry, it's just a blank.'

Hakim patted her arm reassuringly. 'You've done well.' Then, when he realized what he had done, he quickly withdrew his hand. He noticed the nurse hovering outside the room. 'I'd better go.' He stood up and replaced the chair.

'Will you come again?' she asked.

'Of course, if there are any new developments.' He caught her look of disappointment. 'But I'll come anyway,' he added hurriedly. 'To check how you're getting on.'

Anita had just sat down when her office door opened and, totally unannounced, in lumbered Pontus Brodd, who slid his long, wiry frame onto the chair in front of her desk.

'What a pain to be back,' he groaned heavily.

Brodd was the last person Anita wanted to see. To her – and it had to be said, most of her colleagues – Pontus Brodd was a waste of space. Having been foisted onto their team after the deaths of Westermark and Nordlund, he hadn't endeared himself to any of them except Chief Inspector Moberg. He had become Moberg's drinking pal when the chief inspector's third marriage had come to its inevitable end. It was a useful role, as it meant none of the others had to accompany their boss on his routine after-work visits to the nearest bar. However, now that Moberg had found yet another woman – how he had managed this, no one could fathom – Brodd's usefulness was redundant. He was a hindrance. Anita knew exactly why Hakim had rung her about Tord Sundin's murder, even though it was Brodd who was officially on call.

'So, you had a good Christmas?' Anita just wanted him to leave the office and let her get on with chasing up forensics.

'Not bad. Drank a bit too much, if you know what I mean.'

'Sorry, but I've got to get on,' Anita responded impatiently.

'Ah, the *tomten* murder.' Brodd reluctantly entangled himself from the chair. 'Actually, Mirza should have called me in on that Why did he call you?' he added tetchily.

'Probably didn't have your number to hand.' She could see Brodd weighing up whether she was just fobbing him off or not.

'Anything I can do?' he asked without enthusiasm.

'No,' she said almost too quickly. He appeared relieved and ran a hand through his mop of black hair. 'Not yet, anyway.' She found herself being apologetic. 'We're still waiting for the forensics report on Tord Sundin.'

'Fine.' He opened the door, then wavered. 'Did you say Tord Sundin?'

As her hand reached for the office phone, Anita glanced up. 'Yeah, that's the name of the victim.'

'I know that name.'

'I'm surprised.' Her amazement was genuine. 'We couldn't find a criminal record for him.'

'No.' Something was smouldering in that lazy brain of his. 'He hasn't got a criminal record, but the guy who attacked him has.'

Anita was astonished. 'When did this happen?'

'A few years back. I was one of the officers called to the restaurant.'

'What restaurant?'

'Em... it was down in Limhamn. Can't remember the name of it offhand.'

'What happened?'

'One of the employees attacked Sundin. Beat him quite badly. That's why he ended up in prison. This guy, not Sundin.'

'What, one of the staff attacked a diner?'

'No, no, no. Sundin owned the place. He was the chef as well.' Brodd rubbed his brow. 'Now, what did they call the guy? It was... Vest...something. Family originated from one of the Baltic States. Vestermanis! That's it! Ruvin Vestermanis. Did a year for assault.'

'Right, you can do something useful. Dig out the details, and let's see if they throw any light on this case.'

CHAPTER 14

Hakim's phone buzzed just as he reached the hospital entrance. 'Hi Reza, how are you?' Reza was a friend from his school days who now ran a second-hand goods business beyond Värnhem. For a kid from Rosengård, that was the equivalent of being a serious entrepreneur.

'Good. Look, I've got something.' Hakim's ears pricked up. 'You know you came in the other week and asked me to keep an eye out for anything dodgy being offered round here? Well, I had someone in the shop first thing this morning who said she was selling stuff for a friend. Top sound equipment. Big TV. Nearly-new furniture. Even some nice threads.'

'You said "she"?'

'Yeah. A real looker; not one of us.'

'Brunette or redhead?'

He heard Reza chuckle at the other end of the line. 'How did you know? Redhead.' Maybe they were getting somewhere at last. This was the first time that any of the stolen goods had surfaced.

'Did you take any of the stuff?'

'Nope. I don't touch anything hot; you know that.' He sounded deeply offended. But Hakim actually knew his friend only too well. Reza was perfectly capable of fencing the goods and selling them on before calling him.

'Thanks for letting me know. I'm on something else at the moment but I'll try and call in tomorrow; I'll need a description. If she turns up again, get straight back to me.'

'Course, Hakim. Oh, by the way, is that sister of yours still with that white guy?'

'Sorry, mate, you've missed the boat there.' He heard Reza's resigned sigh as he ended the call.

By the time Hakim returned to the polishus, Anita was absorbed in a file. There were two mugs of coffee on the table. Anita nodded at one: 'Thought you'd be back earlier. Might be a bit cold.'

'Thanks.' Hakim took the mug and sat down.

'Any luck with your girlfriend?'

'What girlfriend?' Hakim managed to sound mortified and offended at the same time.

Anita laughed at his discomfort. 'I meant Constable Fogelström.'

'She's going to be all right. Naturally, she was shaken.'

'Naturally.' Anita was amused that Hakim's eyes went everywhere around the room except in her direction.

'The problem is she doesn't remember much. But the two things she can recall is hearing an engine—'

'So, there *was* a vehicle there last night.'

'Yes. That's why she went out to look around. The other thing she remembered was that the door at the back of the barn was open. It's when she went in that everything goes blank.'

Anita drained her coffee and put the mug down with a thud. 'That door was locked this morning and we have the barn keys. So, either the family have duplicates that they haven't told us about, and it was one of them who opened it, or it was someone else entirely who has access to a key. But whoever it was, what were they up to? Why the vehicle? And has any of this got anything to do with Tord Sundin's murder?'

Hakim sipped his coffee then put it down nonchalantly, trying to hide the fact that it was now too cold to drink. 'Did you get onto Eva Thulin?'

Anita gave a little cry of exasperation. 'The poor woman is up to her eyes. We've already buggered up her Christmas, and now there's that shooting down in Kroksbäck. She's promised to get back to me tomorrow, but it'll cost me a good bottle of wine. At least she's upfront about the bribe.'

'So what's that?' Hakim asked with a nod towards the open file on Anita's desk.

'You won't believe this, but Pontus has actually come up with something.' Hakim spread his arms in exaggerated horror. 'I know it only happens once in a blue moon, but...' She picked up a photo from the file and held it for Hakim to examine. The man had neatly combed, thick black hair; was clean-shaven; and had haunted, dark, sunken eyes. The mouth was set firmly. To Hakim, he looked like a man with the weight of the world on his shoulders. 'He's called Ruvin Vestermanis. He's of Latvian-Jewish extraction. Grandparents came over here just before the Nazis occupied their country in 1941.' Anita took the photo back and placed it in the file.

'And why is he of interest?'

'Because Vestermanis ended up in prison for attacking Tord Sundin. Sundin ran a restaurant called The Peacock in Limhamn.'

'The name was in English?'

'Yes. Vestermanis worked there as a waiter. What came out at the trial was that, according to Vestermanis, Sundin picked on him and made his life a misery. One night he just pushed him too far. Vestermanis lost it and attacked him in the kitchen and had to be dragged off by the other kitchen staff.'

'Sundin seems to have had that effect on people.'

'Exactly. But it's got me thinking. If Susanne was right about seeing someone around that afternoon, could it have been Vestermanis?'

'Finishing off what he failed to do last time? Is that likely?' Hakim sounded sceptical.

'Let's go and ask him.'

They drove down to Bunkeflostrand, a modern suburb just south of the Outer Ring Road which ran directly onto the Öresund Bridge. In among the serried ranks of dull, four-storey apartment blocks, they found Ruvin Vestermanis's home. It was with natural reluctance that he let them in. The living room was scantily furnished with second-hand items; its one concession to modernity was a wide-screen TV. On an old chest sat a nine-branched menorah. The clean-shaven Vestermanis of the photo in the file had been replaced by a dishevelled man with several days' growth and tinges of grey in the stubble. His temples were starting to recede; a counterpoint to the rest of his unruly mop of jet black hair, now also with the odd fleck of grey. He was gaunt and didn't look well. They all stood, as it was clear that Vestermanis wanted them out of his apartment as soon as possible.

'We're here about Tord Sundin,' opened Anita. 'You know he's been murdered?'

'Yes. When you sit and watch telly all day, you discover these things.' His voice was gruff, as though it had been forced through a cheese grater.

'We'd like to know where you were on Christmas Eve between three and four in the afternoon.' Anita thought there was no point in beating about the bush.

Vestermanis's anxious eyes flitted between Anita and Hakim. 'You think I killed him? No such luck.'

'Where were you?'

'Waiting for *tomten*.' His laugh was bitter. 'He never turned up. Never does.'

'Here, then?'

'I'm always here. This is the life that Tord Sundin condemned me to.'

'I thought it was you who attacked him.'

He stared at Anita. 'I'm sure you've read my notes. Sundin was a tormentor; a brute who treated his staff like dirt. But a Jew, even a secular one who kept himself to himself, was an even easier target for his bile.'

'So what do you do now?' Anita asked.

'Since I came out of prison, you mean? Well, by that time, my wife was gone, my home was gone. So, I exist. I can't get a job, despite pretending not to be Jewish. You may have noticed that many of us have been driven out of Malmö in recent years.' Anita could understand the reason for his virulence. Vestermanis caught Hakim glancing over at the menorah. 'It reminds me of my parents. If they were alive, we would have been using it for Hanukkah, so we'd have something to celebrate round Christmas.' He fixed Hakim with a glare. 'What do you do to fit in?'

Anita jumped in quickly before Hakim could respond: 'Any witnesses that saw you here?'

'Don't be so stupid. Of course not. Everybody keeps themselves to themselves. This is bloody Sweden.'

Hakim took over. 'The Peacock didn't last long after your attack on Sundin. Less than a year. Was that because of you?'

For the first time, they saw a hint of amusement in his eyes. 'The reason his restaurant went bust had nothing to do with me. Sundin was a dreadful chef. Fine for an old folks' home where they're too gaga to notice the garbage he served up. It was embarrassing at times because the waiting staff had to field all the complaints. It was after I took a dish back that he lost his rag – which was never good at the best of times – and he came out with a stream of nasty comments, mainly to do with not enough Jews being killed in the war. That's why I went berserk. The last straw, you might say.' His voice was perfectly modulated; it was as though the emotion of the event had at last drained away. 'I felt sorry for my co-workers when I heard the place had closed. Working for a pittance, but they needed it. Decent people mainly.' Then almost as an afterthought: 'And herr Thorsson as well.'

Both Anita and Hakim were stunned by the mention of the name. Vestermanis caught their surprise.

'You know him? He was a nice fellow.'

'Yes, but how do you know him? And why feel sorry for him?'

'Because he was Sundin's financial backer. He must have lost a small fortune when the place went bust.'

It wasn't until they were back at the polishus that they seriously discussed their conversation with Ruvin Vestermanis. Both Anita and Hakim had been marshalling their own thoughts on the short drive back. Coffee and a sandwich were helping.

'That puts Thorsson right back in the frame,' said Hakim between munches. 'Even if we make allowance for him not knowing about his wife's fling with Sundin, he can't have been too happy about losing his money. That, plus any suspicion about his wife and Sundin, could quite easily have tipped him over the edge. Tord's coarse remark about Felicia in front of the others could have brought out years of resentment.'

Anita finished her sandwich before replying. 'I have to agree.' 'Oh, by the way, I got confirmation that Susanne did phone her boyfriend, Lucas Drakenberg.' Hakim pulled a piece of paper out of his pocket and squinted at it. 'It was only for two minutes fifty-five seconds and it finished just after four.'

'When she heard her brother discovering the body?'

'Possibly. She wasn't talking to Drakenberg for as long as she indicated. A few calls since, but I suppose that's natural if they're a couple. The question is though: was she really just wandering around outside?'

'Hmmm,' mused Anita. 'And if she was where she said she was, did she really see someone? And was that someone

Vestermanis?'

'So, you're not ruling him out?'

'No. He has motives aplenty, from religious bigotry to losing his wife, home and self-respect. He's got no alibi. The only thing in his favour is that he couldn't have known that Tord was back home.'

'Well... he could have been staking the place out over weeks; months even. Or maybe he just got lucky. Under normal circumstances, the one time he'd expect Sundin to be about is around Christmas.'

Anita had to agree. She picked up the office phone. 'I'm going to call off the round-the-clock police presence. I don't think it'll serve any useful purpose now. And calling it off might even allow the murderer to relax. That could make him or her vulnerable; open to mistakes. We'll start afresh in the morning. Hopefully, Eva Thulin might have something for us.' Hakim started to clear up his sandwich debris. 'Oh, one thing you can do before we call it a day is check if we have anything on Susanne's boyfriend, Lucas Drakenberg. Maybe there was a reason Tord Sundin didn't like him other than that he didn't approve of his daughter hanging about with boys.'

As Anita waited for someone to answer her call, she was already planning another visit to the Thorssons. She might even bring Arne into the polishus. That might put the wind up him. But it was the attack on Constable Fogelström that was still confusing her. What was that all about? Was it linked to Tord Sundin's murder? Or was it something totally unconnected?

CHAPTER 15

Lucas Drakenberg lived on the fourth floor of an apartment close to the intersection of Eriksfältsgatan and Professorsgatan. In the summer, the avenue of trees on Eriksfältsgatan softened the concrete surroundings – in midwinter it was just bare and uninviting. Malmö is a summer city that hides its beauty while hibernating during the colder months. Again, the dreariness made Anita wish that she had gone to Tenerife with Lasse and Jazmin.

Drakenberg answered the door with a weary grunt. He wore stripy boxer shorts, and a black T-shirt which showed off muscled arms, decorated, like Mårten Sundin's, in the cultural warpaint of his generation. He wasn't far off two metres tall, and Anita could see why Susanne was attracted to him; he was handsome, with gelled, short dark hair and a tanned complexion. An unlit cigarette dangled nonchalantly from his mouth. 'You'd better come in,' he said, taking the cigarette out. His air was confident. He was completely unfazed by a visit from the police. Maybe because this wasn't the first time. Hakim had dug up his record: petty thieving as a youth followed by some drug dealing; nothing too heavy, but enough to keep him on the police radar. Recently, he had behaved himself – or not been caught.

They stood in the hallway.

'I suppose you're here about Susanne. I haven't seen her

since the day before Christmas Eve because you've been keeping her under lock and key.'

'It's OK. That's been lifted. You're free to meet up.' He shrugged. 'I just want to know why Susanne's father was unhappy about your relationship with his daughter. I know they argued about you on the day he died.'

He raised an eyebrow. 'I don't know. What's not to like?' Anita couldn't work out if he was being self-deprecating or he really believed it; she suspected the latter. 'Her old man was never around and hadn't twigged that his little girl had grown up and had a mind of her own. Besides, he didn't know how to handle someone like me.'

'Someone with a criminal record.'

He simpered: 'Now, now. I've been straight for a few years, as you well know. I earn an honest living.'

'Doing what?'

'On building sites. How do you think I got these?' he asked as he proudly tapped a bicep with the hand that still had the unlit cigarette clamped between the fingers. 'What I meant, before you started casting unnecessary aspersions, was that someone like me knows how to look after a girl. Perhaps Sundin thought he might lose her.'

'And would he have?'

'Oh, yeah. He was a miserable jerk. Treated the family like his slaves. I treat women with respect. Even older ones.' Anita was staggered that he was actually trying to flirt with her. It was bad enough at any time, but she'd only just had breakfast.

'Susanne phoned you on Christmas Eve around four?'

'That's right.'

'Where were you?'

'At my parents'. Family gathering. Lots of witnesses. Susanne was meant to be there until her dad turned up out of the blue and buggered everything up. But it's all fine now. He can't do that again.'

'And your family can back that up?'

He laughed out loud. 'Why? You think I popped out during *Donald Duck* and killed Susanne's father? Why would Susanne ring me if I was already there?'

'It would give you a convenient alibi. Make it seem you were in one place and not in another.'

'Why would I kill him? I'd already got his daughter. There was nothing he could do about that once he'd fucked off back to his next ship.'

Just then the front door opened behind Anita. She turned round to see a young, dark-haired woman clutching a shopping bag. She gave Drakenberg a worried glance.

'My sister, Alicia. She can tell you where I was on Christmas Eve.'

Alicia Drakenberg still wore a look of suspicion on her pretty face. The family resemblance was now unmistakable. 'Lucas was with us at our parents'. There were about ten people there altogether.'

'Is that enough witnesses for you? We were having a better Christmas than poor Susanne,' grinned Drakenberg as Alicia slid past Anita and her brother and turned into the kitchen. 'I presume that's all.'

'That's all.' Anita turned towards the door and opened it. This had been a fruitless trip, but it was another base covered. Drakenberg hovered at the doorway as she started down the corridor towards the lift. He called after her: 'Come for a drink next time.'

When Anita got to her office, a smiling Eva Thulin was sitting at her desk. Hakim had brought her a coffee.

'Nice Christmas, Eva?'

'No. You lot keep bringing me bodies at the most inopportune times. Just to give you due warning, I've already booked a holiday in Thailand for next Christmas. It was either that or divorce. I prefer the prospect of cold drinks in a hot place to hot arguments in a cold one.'

'I might just join you,' said Anita as she shrugged out of her coat and slung it over the spare chair. 'OK?'

Thulin opened up a file which contained typed sheets of paper and photographs. 'As we haven't got Moberg here, I'll cut through the forensic-speak.' She took out a photo of the back of Tord Sundin lying face down in the snow. 'Well, we know how he died. Bonked on the head. He'd had a lot of alcohol, so I suspect his assailant wouldn't have had to do too much to overcome him.'

'Could a woman have done it?' Anita asked, in the hope that it might narrow the field.

Thulin drummed her fingers on the top of the photograph. 'In the state the victim was in – and I would say the attacker was at least the same size – nearly anybody could have killed him as long as the blow landed in the right place. If someone is motivated or desperate enough, they'll find the strength needed.' She noted Anita's disappointment. 'Sorry to say, I can't rule out a female perpetrator. Anyway, Sundin had his back to the killer and was probably unaware that he was about to be attacked.'

'Which indicates that he knew the person, and that he didn't see them as a threat.'

'Smart boy,' Thulin said with a little bow in Hakim's direction. 'Of course, someone he didn't know might have been hiding close by and might have crept up behind him,' she added. 'But I concede that that's unlikely. Now, I realize you're all agog to know what the murder weapon was. Well, your victim really did land in the soup.' Anita and Hakim appeared nonplussed. 'Sorry, poor joke. Must admit, it's a new one on me; but Tord Sundin was actually killed by soup.'

'What?' spluttered Anita incredulously.

'Seriously. Frozen soup. In a plastic container. I told you I found a strange imprint on his skull that I just couldn't place. But, with my usual genius' – Thulin was in a good mood today – 'and a lot of overtime, I finally worked out that the strange mark came from the bottom rim of one of these.' And as if she were pulling a rabbit out of a hat, Thulin produced a plastic food box from a cool bag that had been out of sight behind the desk. The contents of the box were unidentifiable but had a greenish-white colour. 'I knew you'd have a problem believing me, so I made some soup at home and froze it.' She handed the box to Anita. 'Feel how solid and heavy that is.'

Anita took it and as she felt the weight, she raised her eyebrows in agreement.

'Two solid kilos. Now, take it in both hands and smash Hakim's head with it.'

Holding two corners of the box, Anita stood above the seated Hakim and simulated hitting him on the back of the head. Though she only gave him a tap, his head immediately jolted forward. 'Ow!'

'Imagine that coming down with real power. Blunt force trauma. It fractured the skull casing and fragments made their way into the brain causing haemorrhaging.'

Still clutching the box in her hands, Anita talked directly to Hakim: 'Our murderer must have desperately looked round for something to use, opened the freezer and grabbed the nearest thing to hand.' She turned back to Thulin. 'How on earth do you know it contained soup?' Anita asked with undisguised awe.

'I'm afraid I can't pretend that that was difficult and, I must admit, it also gave me an idea about the container,' Thulin pulled an apologetic face. 'Whoever poured the soup into the box spilt a dribble down the side. Of course, that froze, too. I found traces of it on the victim's head. And in case you're wondering what type of soup it was, it was some kind of fish.'

'Ah!' Hakim exclaimed, slapping his forehead in annoyance.

'Fish soup! That's what they were having two nights ago. They've eaten part of the murder weapon!'

They both stood staring into the half-full freezer with its iced-up sides. Similar boxes to the one Thulin reckoned had been used to kill Tord Sundin were piled up at one side. Anita groaned. 'This is a first. We're going to look bloody stupid when this comes out in court – that's if we get that far.'

Anita let the lid drop and glanced around the barn, trying to recreate the scene in her mind's eye. An inebriated Tord Sundin had come out to the barn to collect his Santa suit and the sack of presents. He'd put the suit on then, possibly, he'd gone into the storage area to look for the missing beard. Someone else was also there. Had that person followed him, or had he arranged to see them and an argument had ensued? Arne Thorsson, Mårten, Elvira and Susanne fell into the first category – with Barbara as an outside possibility. Felicia Thorsson was definitely in the second, with Ruvin Vestermanis as a long shot. Felicia had been heard arguing with Tord after the start of the *Donald Duck* programme. Whoever it was – and they seemed no closer to an answer to that – then waited for Tord to emerge from the storage area, lock it up (the keys were underneath him when he died); and then they improvised a weapon from the freezer. But if he had gone into the storage area, why hadn't he come out with the beard? Or had he seen something else in there that set off the whole tragic train of events? He was taken completely by surprise and probably wouldn't have known what was happening to him. He had gone unmourned. But, however loathsome Tord Sundin had been, it was their job to find his killer.

'What next?' queried Hakim.

'I'll talk to Arne Thorsson and confront him with the new information we have. You can have another word with Elvira. We know she lied about not knowing about the affair. Why? Is she hiding something? And ask her again about that engine she heard. I'd put money on it being the same vehicle that turned up two nights ago.'

Hakim found Elvira in her room working on her laptop – 'Uni work,' she explained as she stifled a yawn. The dark rims around her eyes showed that she hadn't had much sleep lately. Was that due to the fact that she had just lost her father, or was it a guilty conscience?

'Why did you lie to me about not knowing your father was having an affair with Felicia Thorsson?'

'I didn't,' she said irritably as she tore her gaze away from the computer screen which, up until now, had attracted more interest than the presence of the young detective.

'According to your sister, you saw your father and your next door neighbour out in the wood behind here.'

Elvira pursed her lips and exhaled noisily. 'I should never have said anything to Susanne. She can never keep her trap shut.'

'But you did see them?'

She saved something on her computer and then snapped the lid shut. 'Yes I did. It was a betrayal of Mamma.' She did nothing to hide her wrath. 'They were like rutting hogs,' she said with revulsion. 'It was sickening. She's been nothing but trouble since she turned up at Arne's. I bet he's regretting hooking up with her.'

'So, when did this happen? The incident in the wood?'

'Last August. I was home for a few days from Gothenburg. I knew Dad was home and I thought Mamma might need some support. It all depended what sort of frame of mind he was in when he returned. If he'd had a bad voyage, he could be obnoxious. Sometimes he was fine. It was probably because I was around that they sneaked off into the wood.'

'Did you do anything about it, other than tell your sister?'

Elvira stared at Hakim, which suddenly made him self-conscious. Was she weighing him up? Eventually she spoke: 'I had it out with him.'

'You actually raised the subject?'

'Yes.'

There was a long pause as Elvira showed no sign of wanting to enlighten him any further. 'And?' he probed at last.

'And we had a fight. A shouting match. I ended up calling him the most revolting things I could think of and he ended up slapping me. I packed my bags and went straight back to Gothenburg. I emailed some excuse to Mamma about work.'

'So, you didn't tell me this because you were trying to shield your mother?'

'I didn't want it to come out.'

Hakim was still standing by the door. He didn't know what to make of this young woman. 'But don't you think your father's murder might be because of all this?'

'I know,' she said half-heartedly. 'I'm not stupid. I didn't want you to think that I might've had a reason to kill him.'

'But you have.'

CHAPTER 16

Anita had been greeted by Felicia clutching her usual tumbler of gin and a slightly slurred: 'Not you again.' When Anita explained it was her husband she wanted to speak to, Felicia directed her to the outside storehouse. Under a corrugated iron overhang, Arne was neatly splitting a chunk of felled tree trunk. He wielded the axe skilfully. He threw the two resulting logs onto a growing pile before he acknowledged Anita's presence.

'I know, you know,' he said as he wiped his brow. 'About Felicia and Tord. She told me.' He picked up another piece of wood and bisected it perfectly with a well-timed thwack.

'But when did you know?' countered Anita.

Arne leant on his upturned axe.

'Since Christmas Day.'

'Are you sure?'

'You plugging the jealousy motive again? I'm not a blind, lovesick pup. I suspected something might have been going on. I knew what I was taking on with Felicia. She's a woman of the world. I'm just lucky to have her around at my time of life.'

'You didn't seem too happy about things when I came round last time,' Anita pointed out.

'I'd just heard. I admit it hurt my pride to actually hear it said out loud. But we'll survive.'

Anita kicked away a piece of splintered wood with the toe of her brown boot. It skidded across the ground. 'Actually, that wasn't what I came here to speak about. We've been talking to Ruvin Vestermanis.'

'Who?' Then recognition crossed his features. 'The Peacock.'

'Exactly. According to Vestermanis, you lost quite a lot of money in that venture.'

'Not enough to kill someone for. I live comfortably.'

'But now we have a combination of things: Tord dragging you into a bad business venture and you not knowing if he's having an affair with your new wife behind your back. Was Christmas Eve the last straw? The final degradation from a drunken oaf that pushed you over the edge? It would be too much for some men.' She knew she was trying to needle him to get a reaction. The way his hand curled round the handle of his axe was a warning that it might not be the safest of strategies.

Arne picked up another log and with a brutal blow sliced it in half. 'You're barking up the wrong tree, Inspector. Tord Sundin was a nasty, solipsistic brute who got what he deserved. I didn't murder him, though as you've pointed out, I had cause. Now, unless you're going to arrest me, I'd like to finish chopping these logs.'

A thoughtful Anita returned to the Sundins' barn. This case was becoming more exasperating by the minute. She wasn't sure where to turn next. The ridiculous thing was that everyone had motive and opportunity. A maddening thought occurred to her: if they didn't solve this soon, Chief Inspector Moberg would come back from holiday and barge his way into the investigation, making her feel totally incompetent. She chided herself that that was even a consideration. Hardly professional on her part. All the same...

She decided to go back to the beginning. She opened the freezer again -- this was where the murder weapon had come from... Her thoughts were interrupted by someone behind her. She turned round and saw Hakim emerging from the entrance to the storage area. 'While I was waiting for you, I thought I'd have a look.'

'Any ideas?' asked Anita, still holding the freezer lid open. 'I haven't got any.'

'It might be my imagination, but this place seems emptier than the last time I looked in,' Hakim jerked a thumb in the direction of the storeroom.

'What do you mean?'

'Well, I know the light wasn't too good last time I was in there, but I'm sure there were more boxes than there are now. And, what's more, I don't remember this,' and he held up the little ivory figure.

'You wouldn't. I found it on the floor and put it on the table. Thought it might be from one of Tord's trips.'

'I'm not so sure... I've just got to check something.' And Hakim sped out of the barn.

Wearing a puzzled expression, Anita returned to the freezer. It was then that she spotted something. Her heartbeat quickened and she made a concerted effort to keep calm. She fumbled in her black hole of a bag and, after much scrabbling, gave a cry of jubilation as her hand reappeared brandishing a pair of eyebrow tweezers.

As Hakim was about to go into the house, Mårten rode into the yard on his motorbike. He came to a standstill, switched off the engine and took off his helmet. He grimaced when he saw the detective.

'I'd like a word,' said Hakim.

'Look, I've been at work. Early shift. I'm off for a shower,' he said gruffly as he made to wheel his bike through the snow towards the back door of the house. Hakim held up a hand.

'Not just yet. Tell me, does anybody use the barn for storage, other than the family?'

'Not really. Except Lucas Drakenberg. He's used it two or

three times. Just for a few days.'

'What for?'

'Furniture and stuff, I think. He does a bit of house removal on the side.'

'So he's got a key?'

'Must have.'

'And he's got a van?'

'Yeah.'

'Colour?'

'Green effort.'

Hakim returned a wide grin. 'Enjoy your shower.'

Mårten shrugged. Whatever he had said, the Arab inspector appeared happy with it.

Hakim whipped out his phone, quickly punched in a number and waited. 'Pontus, I want you to do something. And before you say anything, I know it's not your case. But just do as I ask,' he said firmly. Then he filled Pontus Brodd in.

Hakim bounced back into the barn. He found Anita squinting through her glasses at something at the end of her tweezers. She walked silently past him and stood in the doorway so she could catch the light.

'What's that?' asked Hakim from behind her.

'It's a wisp of wool. Grey wool. Stuck to the ice on the edge of the freezer.' She turned to face Hakim. 'Not sure if it has any relevance.'

Hakim grabbed Anita's shoulders and gave her a delighted kiss on her cheek. She was as surprised by this sudden burst of affection as he was embarrassed by what he had done. 'Sorry. I'm sorry,' he quickly apologized.

Anita gave him an amused look. 'Don't be. Just tell me why I deserved that.'

He carefully took the tweezers from her grasp and eyed it closely. 'I think you've just found our murderer.'

CHAPTER 17

Susanne wasn't in her room. Barbara Sundin hovered at the door, arms akimbo, as Anita and Hakim went in. 'She's gone out. Anyway, what are you after?'

'The jersey you knitted her for Christmas,' said Hakim distractedly as he looked round the room.

'Why? What do you want it for?' Then seeing Hakim open a drawer, indignation set in: 'Hey, don't you need a search warrant or something? These are my daughter's private things.'

'This is a murder investigation, fru Sundin; we're trying to find your husband's killer. And this may help us eliminate Susanne from our enquiries,' Anita lied. 'Now tell me, when was the first time Susanne wore the jersey?'

Barbara Sundin's voice betrayed both anger and fear: 'I gave it to her on Christmas Eve morning. She put it straight on.'

'Now, this is important. During that day, Christmas Eve, did you at any time send Susanne across to the barn to fetch anything from the freezer?'

'No. Elvira and I got everything out the night before.'

'Here it is!' Hakim announced as he found the unfolded jersey stuffed into a half-open drawer. He held it aloft so Anita could see it.

'You've got what you wanted, now get out!' Barbara was almost in tears.

'I'm sorry, fru Sundin.' Hakim tried to push the drawer shut, but it stuck half way.

'Leave it!' said Barbara, in an attempt to regain control of the situation. In sheer frustration, she grabbed the drawer handle and pulled the whole thing out of its opening. She shoved her arm to the back of the aperture, and a look of bewilderment crossed her features. She withdrew her arm and what she held in her hand made Hakim's heart miss a beat. It was a brunette wig.

Back in the yard, Hakim took a call. Anita saw him listen intently and then say: 'Thanks, Pontus.' He slipped his phone into his pocket

He turned to Anita. 'One last thing. You said when you met Lucas Drakenberg that his sister turned up.'

'That's right.'

'Attractive? Early twenties? About one point seven metres?'

'Yes.'

'But not a redhead?'

'No. Short, dark hair.'

Hakim clasped his hands together in front of his mouth before speaking. 'I believe this is what happened here on Christmas Eve. For starters, I think we got it wrong about the motive. We assumed that our suspects were either jealous or protecting a loved mother; that all fitted in. But, in fact, it had absolutely nothing to do with any of that.'

Anita pulled her coat collar close to her neck. It was very cold now, but she wasn't going to let that get in the way of Hakim's moment of glory. 'OK, go on Kurt Wallander.'

'It's tied up with my robbery case. Three apartments burgled after young, wealthy guys are picked up by two attractive girls in local clubs. The older one a redhead, the younger one a brunette. Except they weren't, because they were wearing wigs. The descriptions the victims gave us were naturally hazy after drinking spiked vodka, but the colour of the girls' hair is the one thing that stuck in their minds and they all agreed on.'

'Drakenberg's sister and his girlfriend?'

'Exactly. I should be able to get a positive ID on the sister from a mate of mine – I'll tell you about that later. Anyway, they drug the men, who don't get their promised threesome, but have their keys duplicated. Then when they're out or away on business, Lucas Drakenberg turns up in his van, presumably with an accomplice, and strips the apartments. They need to store everything before they sell it on. With Tord Sundin away, what's easier than using the barn here? Brodd confirmed that the Japanese ivory figure – it's called a *netsuke*, by the way – was one of the items taken from Greger Sahlén's apartment, which was their last job. Anyway, they would normally have got rid of everything by the time Tord comes back. He'd be none the wiser. The only problem is that he suddenly appears for Christmas throwing everybody's plans into chaos, especially those of Drakenberg and Susanne. They had to move fast. Obviously, they managed to shift a lot of the stolen goods on the night before Tord came back, hence the vehicle Elvira heard. But there were still a number of boxes left: the ones that I saw. So they'd have to wait until Tord went away again, or was out long enough for them to move the rest. They must have just hoped that he wouldn't go in and see what was left.' Anita watched Hakim as his enthusiasm grew, and delighted in the fact that her protégé was really developing into a fine detective.

Hakim started to pace back and forth. 'You can imagine the horror with which Susanne greeted her father's return. It led to the inevitable argument earlier in the day about Drakenberg, whom Tord disliked. But what was worse: she realized that he would want to do his *tomten* bit for Georg. So, she looked out the costume the night before to try and avert her father going into the storeroom. Of course, she didn't realize she'd missed the beard. Anyhow, to be on the safe side, she decided to follow him out. Presumably, she must have overheard him brush off Felicia, and then she hung around the barn. That's why Arne Thorsson didn't see her in the wood on his walk. We can only assume that when Tord actually went into the storeroom looking for the beard, he realized Susanne's worst fears: he would have seen the stolen goods. What would he do? Would he ring the police? Lucas already had a criminal record – this would mean a long spell in jail. And Susanne would also be worrying about what might happen to her. Somehow, she had to stop her dad. Maybe they argued. Anyway, whatever happened, Sundin must have locked the door, leaving the beard behind – presumably that was the last thing on his mind. Remember, he was fairly drunk, and once he'd turned his back on Susanne, he was defenceless. He wouldn't regard her as a threat, as he thought his kids were frightened of him. But he misjudged her. In desperation, she reaches into the freezer and gets hold of the first thing that comes to hand – the container of soup. Inadvertently, her new jersey scrapes against the ice. She hits Tord on the back of his head and the blow kills him. She can't shut the barn door because Tord's body is blocking it, but she turns off the light so that he can't be spotted from the house. She puts the soup back, then heads off to the wood to call Drakenberg to tell him what's happened. He'd know what to do. But she doesn't have much time. We know the call was short and not the long one she claimed.'

'It's all making sense.' By now Anita was beginning to stamp her feet as the cold began to make her toes numb.

'When Susanne is interviewed, she confuses matters by throwing in the possibility of a stranger hanging about, which, ironically, could have been Ruvin Vestermanis. More importantly, with the police sniffing around, it was vital to move the last of the stolen goods out of the barn before we discovered them and started working things out. Of course, you complicated things by ensuring a police presence was here all the time. Drakenberg and Susanne must have decided that desperate measures were required. They were about to move everything out when poor

Liv Fogelström stumbled across them.' Anita noticed that Hakim's voice softened at the mention of Fogelström's name. 'Despite that, they get the stolen items away, but miss the *netsuke*; probably fell out of a box and was too small to notice in their hurry.' Hakim had now run out of steam.

'Very good, Inspector Mirza. All we have to do now is prove it. Prosecutor Blom will want watertight evidence before we're allowed to arrest anybody. I suggest the first thing we do is find Drakenberg and Susanne, and have a *real* talk.'

CHAPTER 18

They drove back into Malmö and headed for Lucas Drakenberg's apartment; that's where Susanne had gone, according to Barbara. The *netsuke* was in a plastic evidence bag in Anita's pocket. She was undecided at this stage whether to confront Drakenberg and Susanne with this. She would play it by ear. She knew she couldn't arrest them without a prosecutor's say-so, but she didn't want to waste time. Was it the thought of Moberg's imminent return that made her want to speed things up? Thanks to Hakim, they were now reasonably sure who had done what and when – and why. She wanted to present him as the hero of the hour to the chief inspector.

They turned off the Inner Ring Road and into the Östra Söderkulla district. A couple of minutes later, Anita drew up at the kerb close to Drakenberg's apartment building. They got out of the car and walked towards the front entrance. On reaching the apartment, Anita pressed the buzzer. No one answered. She tried again before banging on the door. Nothing. 'Not in,' she growled disappointedly. Back in the car, they decided to wait a while and see if the pair returned. They sat in silence, each lost in their own thoughts. Anita's drifted to Tenerife and wondered how Lasse and Jazmin were getting on.

She was brought out of her reverie by a nudge from Hakim. 'That's them.' A large green transit van turned into the street off Eriksfältsgatan and came to a standstill. Lucas Drakenberg jumped out from the driver's side; the passenger door opened and Susanne appeared. As Drakenberg was about to lock the van, Anita and Hakim emerged and she called over: 'Can we have a word?'

Panic immediately crossed Susanne's face and she stayed close to the van, but Drakenberg just smiled, his right hand still holding his key fob in mid-air. 'They've tracked you down, babe,' he said playfully. 'Or is it me you want to speak to? Can't get enough of young men?' He winked towards Hakim.

'We want to speak to both of you.'

'Who have we supposedly murdered now?'

'It's not that. It's about the apartments you've been emptying, with the help of Susanne and your sister.'

The cockiness immediately drained out of Drakenberg. He tried to force a blasé smile, but his face betrayed unease. 'Don't know what you're talking about.' Susanne looked on fearfully.

'When you attacked that police constable, you left one item behind.'

'Nah, we...' Drakenberg's eyes whipped from the detectives in front of him to his apartment building and to the van.

'Now, can we have that word?'

Drakenberg suddenly shouted: 'Get in, babe!' He yanked open the driver's door before Anita and Hakim could react. He managed to start the engine as Susanne scrambled into the passenger seat. Hakim was pulling at the handle of the van door when the vehicle shot away, nearly throwing him off his feet.

'Quick!' Anita yelled as she rushed back to her car, and by the time Hakim was at her side, they were moving. She gunned the engine and took after the transit, which was squealing around the corner at the end of the street. The aging Peugeot wasn't the world's most effective pursuit vehicle, but she got enough out of it to keep Drakenberg's van in sight. The two vehicles rattled along the roads, which were virtually empty as it was still the holiday period. The afternoon was becoming murkier and the first flakes of a fresh snowfall began to float lazily out of the dark-yellow sky, forcing Anita to use her rather uncooperative windscreen wipers.

'Shall I call for back-up?' Hakim clutched his phone on his lap ready for use.

'In a minute. I don't know where he's heading.'

As the van careered round a bus at a stop, Anita had to take evasive action as the bus started to pull out into the road. She swore at the driver, who hooted back. When the van shot straight under the Inner Ring Road roundabout, it became clear that Drakenberg was either heading south onto the E6, or onto the E20 and the Öresund Bridge.

'Call in any patrol cars in the vicinity,' Anita ordered as she tried to extract the maximum power from her reluctant vehicle. Already there were two cars between them and their quarry as the more powerful transit wove its way through the traffic. The snow was now falling more rapidly, which was making it harder to see through the windscreen. As Hakim barked instructions into his mobile, Anita was kicking herself for getting into this situation in the first place. If they had got the couple into the apartment first, they would have stayed in control. Now it was potential mayhem – she just hadn't envisaged Drakenberg making a bolt for it. She cursed herself again as she saw the van veering off the dual carriageway. 'It's the Bridge!' she shouted, as she screwed up her eyes to see through the gloom. 'Get cars out there to stop them. They'll try and ram through and get across to Denmark.'

Now it was a straight chase. The traffic thickened on the approach to the toll booths. A sudden wind had whipped up, and the snow was now horizontal, blurring her vision.

'They're getting away, Anita!'

'I bloody know!' she said through gritted teeth as more vehicles came between them and the van.

Anita leant forward over the steering wheel, willing her car to go faster. 'Where the hell is the back up?' she screamed in frustration as there was no sign of a reassuring police siren.

Even with her wipers going at full speed, they could hardly keep up with the lively dance of the snowflakes on the windscreen, but Anita knew they were getting close to the bridge. Their quarry was now lost in the traffic ahead. She jammed her foot down on the accelerator to coax the last effort out of a car she was mentally consigning to the scrapheap. 'We're going to lose them,' muttered Hakim darkly. Anita stifled a yell of exasperated admonishment. Of course they were losing them!

Ahead, the toll signs appeared through the blizzard, and vehicles were starting to slow down as they approached the serried ranks of booths underneath their metal canopy. Now they could just make out the van as it veered away from the queuing traffic and headed to an unmanned booth at the far end of the row. Drakenberg was showing no signs of slowing down. 'There!' shouted Hakim. Myriad blue streaks of light, refracted by the snow on the windscreen, alerted them to a patrol car which had been parked at the edge of the plaza, and was now roaring across the oncoming traffic, siren blaring, in an effort to intercept the van. Drakenberg tried to swing his vehicle away from the police car without reducing his speed.

'Oh, Christ!' Anita cried as she could see exactly what was about to happen. The van skidded, sending waves of slush and snow across the tarmac. It smashed into the unoccupied booth. For an instant, time was suspended; even the snowflakes seemed caught in a trance. Then an ear-splitting explosion ripped the air.

An hour later, some semblance of order was being restored. There were still half a dozen police cars and three fire engines parked at the scene, which was illuminated by the lights above the toll plaza. As the snow continued to swirl around them,

Anita could see that the huge traffic jam that had built up behind them was at last being slowly funnelled through a booth that hadn't been closed. Fortunately, no one else had been hurt, but there wasn't much left of Lucas Drakenberg and Susanne Sundin to take away. Anita sighed – she knew there would be hell to pay when Moberg got back. The commissioner would be apoplectic. All this public chaos because she was caught off her guard. What a horrible Christmas this was turning out to be; she should have stayed at her mother's!

'Come on,' she said to Hakim. 'Nothing more we can do here. I'll drive you back.'

'Can you drop me at the hospital?' he asked sheepishly.

'To see your girlfriend?' she teased.

'Liv's not my girlfriend. But she needs to know why she was attacked and all the rest...' he tailed off.

They walked across to Anita's car, which was now covered in snow. What an old crock! but she knew she wouldn't get round to changing it. Her mobile abruptly buzzed in her pocket. 'Please, God, let it be something good,' she muttered as she took out the phone. When she saw it was Lasse, her face lit up.

'Hi, Sweetheart, how are you?'

'Hi, Mamma. Still at Grandma's?'

'No. Long story. Having a good time?'

'Brilliant.'

Anita wiped the snow off her glasses. There was a pause at the other end, which made her immediately wary. She could always sense when her son had something on his mind.

'Lasse, is anything wrong?'

'No. No. Not at all.'

'What is it? Spit it out.'

There was another pause. 'Mamma, how do you fancy becoming a granny?'

Christmas suddenly just got a whole lot better.

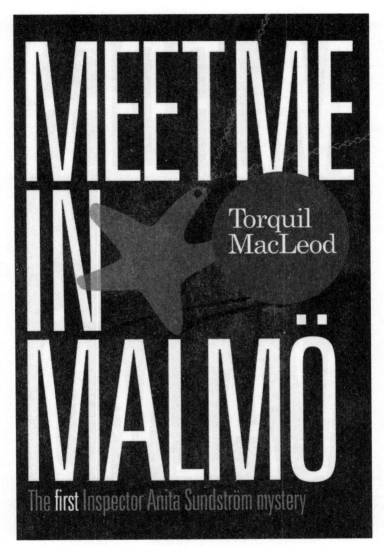

MEET ME
IN
MALMÖ

Torquil
MacLeod

The first Inspector Anita Sundström mystery

ISBN 9780857161130

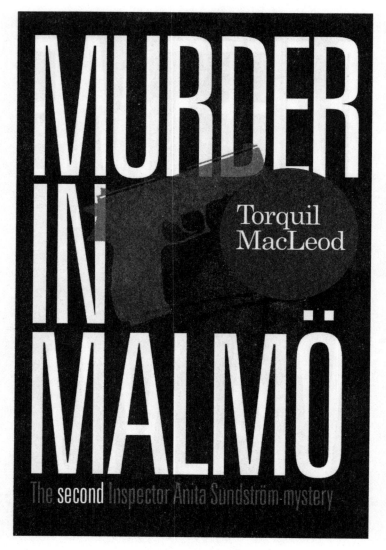

MURDER
IN
MALMÖ

Torquil
MacLeod

The second Inspector Anita Sundström mystery

ISBN 9780857161147

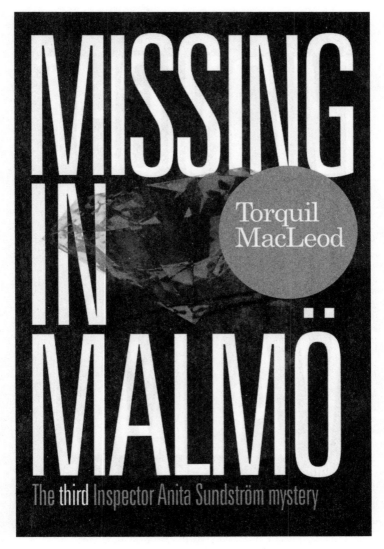

MISSING IN MALMÖ

Torquil
MacLeod

The **third** Inspector Anita Sundström mystery

ISBN 9780857161154

MIDNIGHT
IN
MALMÖ

Torquil
MacLeod

The fourth Inspector Anita Sundström mystery

ISBN 9780857161307

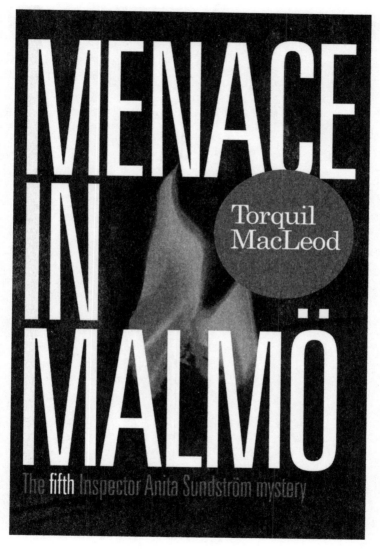

MENACE IN MALMÖ

Torquil
MacLeod

The fifth Inspector Anita Sundström mystery

ISBN 9780857161734